NEW KIDS

&

UNDER DOGS

Also by Margaret Finnegan

Susie B. Won't Back Down
We Could Be Heroes

NEW KIDS

&

UNDER DOGS

Margaret Finnegan

ATHENEUM BOOKS FOR YOUNG READERS
New York London Toronto Sydney New Delhi

ATHENEUM BOOKS FOR YOUNG READERS

An imprint of Simon & Schuster Children's Publishing Division

1230 Avenue of the Americas, New York, New York 10020

Text © 2022 by Margaret Finnegan

Jacket illustration © 2022 by Karyn Lee

Jacket design by Karyn Lee © 2022 by Simon & Schuster, Inc.

ATHENEUM BOOKS FOR YOUNG READERS is a registered trademark of Simon & Schuster, Inc. Atheneum logo is a trademark of Simon & Schuster, Inc.

For information about special discounts for bulk purchases, please contact Simon & Schuster Special Sales at 1-866-506-1949 or business@simonandschuster.com.

The Simon & Schuster Speakers Bureau can bring authors to your live event. For more information or to book an event, contact the Simon & Schuster Speakers Bureau at 1-866-248-3049 or visit our website at www.simonspeakers.com.

Interior design by Karyn Lee

The text for this book was set in Droid Serif.

Manufactured in the United States of America

0922 FFG

First Edition

10 9 8 7 6 5 4 3 2 1

Library of Congress Cataloging-in-Publication Data

Names: Finnegan, Margaret, 1965– author. | Title: New kids and underdogs / Margaret Finnegan. | Description: First edition. | New York : Atheneum Books for Young Readers, [2022] | Audience: Ages 8–12. | Audience: Grades 4–6. | Summary: "Ten-year-old perpetual new kid Robyn has rules about starting a new school, but she learns some rules are worth breaking when she signs up her special needs dogs for agility training"—Provided by publisher.

Identifiers: LCCN 2021055551 | ISBN 9781534496408 (hardcover) | ISBN 9781534496422 (ebook)

Subjects: CYAC: Dogs—Training—Fiction. | Animals with disabilities—Fiction. | Friendship—Fiction. | Schools—Fiction. | LCGFT: Novels.

Classification: LCC PZ7.1.F53684 Ne 2022 | DDC [Fic]—dc23

LC record available at https://lccn.loc.gov/2021055551

To Steve

CHAPTER 1

ROBYN KELLEN STEPPED OUT of the car and stared at her new home. It was not much to look at. A small, boxy house covered in stucco, with gravel and succulents where a front lawn should have been. But there was a palm tree. People had promised California would have palm trees. And, sure enough, San Luis Obispo—a town at once beachy, woodsy, and restaurant-y—seemed to have more than a few.

"Let's get you inside," said Mom, pulling Robyn's suitcase from the trunk. "The dogs will be so excited to see you!"

Robyn smiled. She was excited to see them too. She liked spending her summers with her dad, his partner, and her half brother, Joshua, but nothing—*nothing*—compared to coming home to a dog. And she had two of them: Sundae and Fudge, three-year-old Jack Russell terrier mixes with wiry white-and-brown fur, floppy ears, and curly tails. They went wild every time she returned from the grocery store. So how did they react when she came back from a lengthy stay at her dad's?

How does an athlete react upon winning an Olympic gold medal? How does a lottery winner react upon winning millions of dollars? Combine those reactions and multiply them by ten. *That* was how Sundae and Fudge behaved whenever Robyn returned from her dad's. At least it seemed that way.

And who would not be eager to soak up that love?

Robyn followed Mom into the house.

At first, there was quiet. And in that moment Robyn was able to get a glimpse of her new home. To the left, the doorway to the kitchen. She could just make out the corner of the stainless-steel sink. Straight ahead, the living room, looking oddly familiar with the beige couch and the flowered armchairs that had been with Robyn and Mom for at least the last three moves.

And then came the clickety-click-clack of dog nails pounding against hardwood flooring. Sliding and scrambling as he rounded the corner and picked up speed was Sundae, his eyes eager to see if his nose was right, if he really had smelled Robyn. As always, behind him came Fudge, taking it easy, trusting her nose completely.

"Sundae! Fudge!" called Robyn as they bulldozed into her, knocking her off-balance and making her drop the two carry-on bags in her hands. Barking erupted as Sundae began jumping, springlike, as high as Robyn's face. He flicked out his tongue and got a little taste of her cheek. Fudge circled Robyn and howled.

Robyn plopped onto the floor as the stress and numb tiredness of her long journey—the five-hour flight from Toronto, the three-hour drive from Los Angeles to the Central Coast—fell away. Her eyes grew bright as the dogs squirmed around her, their curled tails vibrating like possessed maracas. They licked her face. They licked her arms. And when they were finally done with the licking, they collapsed upon her and gave her grateful, adoring, pleading looks that begged her to never part from them—her pack—again.

She felt a little guilty. She always did. This was the cost of such a hero's welcome: the knowledge that her absence had pained them so much.

So she petted them, and cooed at them, and kissed their pink little noses, until—reassured that Robyn was here to stay—they waddled over to the kitchen, where they sat down in front of a cupboard right inside the doorframe. Tired from the excitement, Fudge dropped her belly on the floor. Sundae stared up at the cupboard door.

"I guess that's where you keep the treats," said Robyn.

Mom sighed. "I tried keeping them in the pantry, but they figured out how to open it."

Robyn got up. "Oh, you guys are so smart, aren't you? My sneaky little geniuses, huh?" She walked over to the cabinet and pulled down the treat bag. She gave one treat to each dog.

Sundae swallowed his and immediately stared back up at the bag.

But Fudge, polite and grateful to the core, bumped her backside against Robyn's calf and ran her tongue across Robyn's shoe. If that wasn't a thank-you, Robyn didn't know what was.

Robyn pulled her new phone out of her pocket, took a picture of the dogs, and texted it to Dad. She had promised him lots of pictures of Sundae and Fudge and her everyday life. And since it was the promise of such pictures that had finally convinced him to get her her own phone, she was not going to let him down.

Mom had not been happy to see that phone when Robyn showed it to her, and since Mom had never budged in her resistance to letting Robyn have a phone, that hadn't been a surprise. But, as Robyn had hoped, the joy of a mother-daughter reunion outweighed any reservations about the phone. Mom hadn't said a word about it on the drive home. And she didn't say anything about it now.

Instead, Mom offered Robyn a tour of the house. Since there were only two bedrooms and one bathroom, it did not take long.

When they came to Robyn's room, Mom said, "Feel free to rearrange stuff. You do you."

Robyn glanced around. The room was smaller than the one she'd had in Portland, and the view—a tiny yard with browning grass—was less attractive than the one she'd had in Boulder. But it was kind of cute. While the walls were off-white, the ceiling was painted the same sea green as her comforter, and there was a little arch over the door to her closet.

Her things were just where she would have put them herself. Tutu Tiger was propped against her pillow. Her favorite books were categorized on her bookshelf—old picture books in one area; favorite chapter books in another; books about science, animals, and the natural world in a third. And, of course, her cracked ceramic elephant lamp was on her dresser. She knew the lamp was a little babyish now that she was ten, but she didn't think she'd ever have the heart to get rid of it. It had been loyal to her all these many years and many moves. She would be loyal to it in return.

Most importantly, the dogs were lying on her bed, watching her, and she could hear Mom rummaging around in the kitchen. And that was what made her feel at home more than anything. Robyn looked around the room once more and smiled grimly when she saw her old bulletin board hanging above her desk. With a sigh, she grabbed the smaller of her two carry-ons, opened it, and dug around for the journal her dad had given her the day before.

"Write whatever you want in here," he'd said upon handing it to her. He'd been holding Joshua, who—acting like the grabby one-year-old he was—instantly lunged for it.

But two straight months with Joshua had taught Robyn a thing or two. She snatched the journal before Joshua could get it, and she turned sideways as she admired the illustration of a palm tree on the front.

"For California," Dad had said excitedly.

She'd nodded. "For California."

Now actually *in* California, she opened the journal and carefully tore out the list she'd spent so much time writing and thinking about during her flight. She dropped her chin. It was a good list. It was very scientific and, therefore, factual. Everything on it was based on the *law of cause and effect*, which her class had learned about in fourth grade. If you leave ice in the sun, it will melt. If you mix yellow and blue, you will get green. If you give a plant the right amount of water, sunlight, and good-enough soil, it will grow.

Still, it wasn't until the summer that she began

to apply the law of cause and effect to her own life, and it was all thanks to Joshua. Joshua *was* cause and effect. If he had a messy diaper, he cried. If someone changed him, he stopped. If he was hungry, he cried. If someone fed him, he stopped.

But, really, how different was Joshua from anyone else? She'd wondered that one day when Joshua fell over, banged his head against the carpet, and started to cry, and then Dad—in picking him up—banged his own head against the wall and looked like he might start crying too. It made her think: Weren't we all just banging our heads against walls and then paying the consequences? Indeed, hadn't every encounter—good and bad—at every school in every town she'd ever lived in proved that very lesson? The friends she'd made. The friends she'd failed to make. The school subjects she'd aced. The ones she hadn't. Weren't they all the results of unseen causes and effects, actions and reactions?

That was a depressing thought.

But did it have to be? This was the *new* thought that occurred to her somewhere over the Rocky Mountains. Once again, it was because of Joshua. She'd been remembering saying goodbye to him. His face had begun to strain and turn purple—a sure sign that he was midpoop. Lickety-split, they changed him before he could make a fuss. They'd been getting better at that—at reading his signals—and in doing so, they were learning this important, undeniable life lesson about cause and effect: poop happens, but if you are prepared, you can minimize the worst of it.

So . . . couldn't she do the same? San Luis Obispo would be the sixth city Robyn and her mom lived in—the sixth time Robyn would be the new kid in school. Couldn't she minimize the worst of being a new kid? Poop would happen. That was inevitable when you moved someplace new. But by reading the signs and sending the right signals, couldn't she make it easier? Couldn't she gain some control over the matter?

If that was the case, what would that control look like? How could she possibly prepare for it? Aha! That was the easy part. That was the science experiment she had unknowingly been living her whole life. So she'd pulled out her journal on the plane, put down her tray table, and got to work. She made a list that pulled together all the lessons of all those moves, one that would allow her to do what no new kid had ever done before: transition seamlessly and without drama into a new school.

And now, in her new room, she secured the list to the bulletin board.

Hands on her hips, she stood and read it:

Rules for New Kids

To be followed as closely as possible. DO NOT
   IGNORE!
1. Don't stand out. Lay low and *blend in*.
2. People are judgers, so don't make it easy for
   them to judge you.
3. Fight fire with fire—*if absolutely necessary*—but
   don't burn down the whole school.
4. Laugh it off. *Whatever it is,* laugh it off.
5. Don't go looking for trouble.
6. Stay busy. Don't look alone.
7. Be nice to everyone.
8. Don't rush things.
9. If they hurt you, don't let it show.
10. Be flexible.
DO THESE THINGS AND EVERYTHING WILL TURN
   OUT FINE!

"Cause and effect," she said softly to Sundae and
Fudge. "Do the right action to get the right reaction.
It's going to work. It *has* to work."

CHAPTER 2

ROBYN BELIEVED THAT A new town should be approached like a wild, unpredictable animal. Appreciate its charms, but don't get too attached. It was something she'd learned from all those moves. The moves were a consequence of Mom's job as a university biology professor. For years, she'd been bumping between one-year research projects and teaching gigs, which meant she would pack up their things when one school year ended and unpack somewhere new when another school year began. Robyn, who was usually with her dad when all this was happening, would arrive just in time to start her own new school year in her own new school.

But San Luis Obispo was supposed to be different. San Luis Obispo was supposed to be permanent. If Mom published enough of her research and did a good-enough job teaching her students, she might work at the university in San Luis Obispo for the rest of her career. That, in itself, was the reason for Robyn's rules. As science and Joshua proved, cause and effect always mattered, but they especially mattered when there were no do-overs, and there would be no do-overs in new schools and new towns if they never left this one. What happened to Robyn in San Luis Obispo—who she was in San Luis Obispo—might follow her for the rest of her days.

But as different as San Luis Obispo was supposed to be, it was already beginning to feel like everywhere else. And it wasn't just because of the dogs, or Mom, or the furniture, or the arrangement of her room. It was the other little things that added structure to her life.

There was Trader Joe's, where they went on Robyn's first full day in San Luis Obispo. She was tired from the time change and Fudge's constant habit of hogging the bed, but Trader Joe's is Trader Joe's, and—tired or not—she knew just where to find the Joe-Joe's cookies.

There was Robyn's school, which they drove past on the way back from buying groceries. It was an easy walk from her house and looked a lot like her Portland school, one story, flattish roof, with a Little Free Library out front and a big board for posting PTA announcements.

There was the babysitter, who came and met her that afternoon. As usual, she was a university student. As usual, she wore jeans. Her name was Nivien.

She had long red nails that she used to tuck her dark hair into a head scarf. She seemed nice enough. Then again, the babysitters were always nice enough. But babysitters were a lot like new towns, in Robyn's opinion. It was best to appreciate their charms and not get too attached.

And, of course, there was the question of extracurriculars. Mom loved extracurriculars. She was always taking up activities and eager for Robyn to do the same. In Boulder, Mom had learned to ski and make bread. In Portland, she had tried hiking and French lessons. It was only a matter of time before she found some new ways to entertain herself in San Luis Obispo, but it was *not* a matter of time before she asked Robyn to do the same. It was, as it always was, one of the first things Mom wanted to address.

She brought it up after Nivien left and they were walking the dogs. They had gone to the park near their house. It was a nice, big park. It had picnic tables, a playground, tennis courts, plenty of open space, and a path that wound its way between all these inviting spaces.

They had barely entered the park when Mom said, "So, what sounds fun these days? I've been exploring your options. There's a creator space that seems neat. And I hear there is a very good judo studio not too far from here. Oh! And get this, there is a farm where you can help raise livestock. I know how much you love animals."

Suddenly, all Robyn wanted to do was go back to sleep. It was not that she was opposed to after-school activities. She'd actually liked some of them, like the cooking class she'd taken in Boulder and the Humane Society camp she'd gone to in Portland. But, jeez, let a kid dip their toes in the pool first. She'd only just arrived. Planting her feet firmly on the ground, she said, "No. No activities. I just got here."

Mom made a growly sort of humming sound. "I won't rush you, but people need activities."

A sudden burst of loud barks—deep, big-dog barks—drew their attention toward the far side of the path. As they got closer, they could see what was going on. A line of adults—each paired with a leashed dog—stood watching the instructor, a solidly built woman with silver hair. The woman had a dog too. It was enormous. Robyn might have thought it a pony but for its short neck and fluffy white fur. It lay at the woman's side, unleashed and asleep.

A boy with shaggy dark hair stood next to the woman. His arms were crossed, and he nodded as she spoke, as if fully endorsing her message.

Robyn's eyes moved past him to take in the broader scene. It seemed obvious that she was looking at a dog-training class, but it was like no dog-training class she had ever seen before. One by one, the woman was having the dog owners guide their dogs through an obstacle course that included hurdles, tire swings, balance beams, seesaws, tunnels, and more.

Unable to keep her eyes off the activity, Robyn said, "What's that?"

"Oh," said Mom. "That's agility dog training. It's cool, isn't it?"

Both dogs' nostrils were dancing, and Sundae let out a little whine.

Robyn had heard the phrase "love at first sight" before. Usually, it was when she and Mom were streaming an old princess movie. They would be having a good time, and then the prince and the princess would meet each other and get all googly-eyed, and Mom would say something like, "Don't be fooled, Robyn. Love doesn't work that way. There is no such thing as love at first sight." It was always a little unsettling, frankly. It seemed so random. It wasn't like Robyn was listening for love bells or getting ready to elope. But lo and behold, Mom was wrong. Love at first sight did exist! And this was it. And by the way Sundae and Fudge were pulling on their leashes, she could tell they agreed.

She pointed at the obstacle course. "I changed my mind. I'll do an after-school activity. I'll do *that*."

She imagined herself guiding Sundae and Fudge

through the obstacles, seeing them leap and run and balance their ways across the awesome course. She'd be with her dogs. She'd be teaching them things, and they'd be loving on her, and she would never get tired of it. Just as good: she wouldn't have to deal with any judgey kids, just judgey adults, and judgey adults were so much easier. Judgey adults thought you were cute, even if you messed up, and if they didn't think you were cute, they usually kept their opinions to themselves.

"Honey," said Mom. "You can't do agility training. That's impossible."

Shock spread across Robyn's face. Mom had just said she wanted Robyn to find an activity, and now here she was saying no to the best activity Robyn had ever seen, the first activity Robyn had actually volunteered for.

"Why?" It was the only word Robyn could utter.

Mom drew back her head like *she* was the confused one. "Well . . . because of Sundae and Fudge."

Robyn drew back her own head. "What about Sundae and Fudge?"

"Robyn," said Mom. "Fudge is deaf, and she can only see about a foot in front of her."

This was true. It had been true for as long as they'd had Fudge. There was a whole story behind it, one that Robyn would haul out when necessary, but it was hardly ever necessary because Fudge's disabilities never stopped her from doing anything. She had a great nose for figuring things out. Literally. She could smell where the furniture was. She could smell how high to jump to get on Robyn's bed. And when in doubt, Fudge had Sundae to guide her. Sundae never let himself get more than a few feet away from Fudge.

Robyn gave Mom a look of complete bafflement.

In return, Mom gave Robyn her own look of bafflement. "And Sundae is terrified of doing anything without Fudge."

That was also true. There was a story behind that too—the same one as Fudge's. But Sundae's dependence on Fudge mattered even less than Fudge's disabilities. Because as long as the dogs did this agility-training sport together, they would be fine. Sundae—with his perfect eyes and ears—would go first over the hurdles and through the tire swings and everything else. Fudge would follow behind him. She would do what he did. She would just do it a split second later. It was what she mostly did now. And with her presence to boost his confidence, they would both be unstoppable. This had all been so instantly obvious to Robyn that she was convinced Mom was lying to her.

"You just don't want me to have any fun," said Robyn.

Mom waved at the course. "That's not true. Think about it. Fudge would fall off half the things out there. She could get hurt. And Sundae won't get near any of it without Fudge. If we had different dogs, I would be all for it. But we have the dogs we have, and I love the dogs we have, and I want to keep the dogs we have safe. So, no."

Robyn raised her hands in the air, ready to argue, but Mom had her. That was the problem with having a science-minded mom: she worked with cold, hard facts, just like Robyn. Not knowing how to respond, Robyn dropped her hands to her sides, speechless.

Mom continued on the path.

Robyn, both dog leashes in her hand, fell in behind her. She watched the agility class until they were fully past it, and she knew for a fact that Sundae and Fudge were watching it too. That's right, even Fudge was watching. She was watching with her nose. Oh, those dogs were as in love with agility as much as she was. Robyn could tell.

Robyn stopped again. She said, "Wait," and her mother turned around.

"It's not fair. You're not a dog expert. And you always say we should listen to experts about the things they're expert in. The dog trainer is the expert. I should at least get to ask *her* if Sundae and Fudge can take agility."

A half smile crept onto Mom's mouth. She motioned toward the instructor. "Well argued. Fine. Go ahead. Ask her."

The class was beginning to wrap up, so they waited a few minutes, and when the students (both human and dog) began to drift away, Robyn walked with Sundae and Fudge over to the teacher.

She said, "Excuse me, I was wondering if I could maybe sign my dogs up for one of your classes."

The boy and the big white dog ambled over. The boy scratched the dog as he watched Robyn out of the corner of his eye.

The lady took a good look at Sundae and Fudge before turning back to Robyn. "Maybe. Have they done agility before?"

Robyn shook her head no. Then, politely and directly, she explained her situation.

It seemed to go well.

The woman looked concerned when Robyn said Fudge was deaf and vision-impaired, but then the woman looked happy when Robyn said that Fudge's disabilities shouldn't matter because, as a young dog full of pep, Fudge could do basically anything. And the woman looked even happier when Robyn said Sundae could see and hear perfectly, and that that was why she wanted to train the two dogs together.

"But the problem," said Robyn, "is my mom." She motioned to her mother. She was standing under a tree, and when she saw Robyn and the woman looking at her, she gave a little wave.

Robyn continued. "My mom has this silly idea that Sundae and Fudge can't do agility training."

Without a blink, without a breath, the woman pushed out her lips and said, "Your mother is right. Agility isn't the right sport for them."

Robyn fell back. How was this possible? It was as if Mom and the woman had been working together, telepathically, just to deny her. But that couldn't be. Robyn glanced at the boy. He'd crossed his arms, and he was looking with interest at Sundae and Fudge.

"B-but . . . ," stammered Robyn. "They're very smart dogs. They can learn things."

"I'm sure you're right," said the woman. She walked over to a hurdle and began to dismantle it, dropping the bar onto the ground before moving to a second hurdle. She stopped and turned around, glanced at Sundae. "Now, if you can manage to get his anxiety under control, *he* might be able to do agility."

Robyn came closer. She wrinkled her nose. "He doesn't have anxiety. He just likes to be with Fudge."

The woman was already walking again. She reached a nylon tunnel and started to collapse it. "It's nothing personal, dear."

Robyn felt a tug on the leash and looked down to find Fudge standing directly underneath the giant white dog's belly. The beast could have squashed Fudge like a bug if it wanted to, but Fudge could tell, same as Robyn, that this was the most relaxed, Buddha-like being on the planet.

Sundae was not so sure. He stood a way back, his neck craned so that he could smell the big dog without getting near it. He let out a short, panicked "Ruff," and his tail slid between his legs.

Robyn felt like letting out a short, panicked "Ruff" of her own. She could not believe this was happening. Surely this woman—a dog expert, a dog lover—could not have rejected Robyn and her dogs so quickly.

Desperate, Robyn turned to the boy. Maybe *he* would understand. "Sundae and Fudge just want to have fun. They just want to do what other dogs do."

He looked up at her with soulful, caring eyes.

She bit down on her lip, silently begging him to stand up to the woman, make her see reason.

Instead, he said, "Please mooove." He said it like that. Like he was talking to a cow. "You're standing on a hurdle."

She glanced and saw the hurdle bar beneath her feet. Then she stepped away. She glanced back at Mom, whose expression was sympathetic, but also a tiny bit victorious.

Robyn sighed. Cause and effect could be a real jerk sometimes.

CHAPTER 3

"'**AGILITY.' IT'S JUST SUCH** a good word," Robyn said to Sundae and Fudge the next morning. She was getting ready for the inevitable—the first day of fifth grade—while actively, insistently, trying not to think about it. "*A-gil-i-ty*. It sounds like a flavor of Italian ice cream or a fancy kind of restaurant potatoes."

She had let the dogs out and given them their breakfast. Now they were in the living room. She spoke to them through the kitchen door as she made her breakfast.

"Personally, I think you were born for agility training and have every right to give it a try. Don't you agree?" She picked up a banana and began to slice it with a butter knife.

She looked through the doorframe to see Sundae walking straight across the top of the couch. It was just like he was on one of those doggy balance beams she'd seen in the park. Fudge was right behind him.

"Exactly. You really want me to find a way to make it happen. Give me time. I'll work on it after school."

She put the banana slices atop a piece of bread spread thickly with peanut butter. Just then a flutter began to upset her tummy.

Ignoring it, she said, "I wonder what that word 'agility' means, anyway."

She stopped. Listened to make sure she could still hear Mom using the bathroom sink. Then she pulled out her phone and quickly looked up the word's definition. It was a dicey move. The kitchen had been declared a no-phone zone. That's right. Mom—who had stayed so calm when Robyn had pulled out her new Dad-gifted phone—was now wreaking her revenge, declaring places left and right no-phone zones. Besides the kitchen, she had banned Robyn from using her phone in her bedroom, the bathroom, and the car.

"Hmmm," said Robyn, refusing to admit that the flutter had turned into a definite sort of squeezing sensation. "'Agility.' It means you can move quickly and with ease." She put a second piece of bread on top of the first and took a bite of her sandwich. "Duh, of course you can."

But that pain in her belly was persistent. And tricky. Seeing that she would not acknowledge it as a flutter or a squeeze, it transformed into molten lead that weighed down her stomach, then her thighs, and then her calves.

"It's completely unfair, Mom!" she yelled. By this time, she was in her bedroom putting shoes on her heavy feet. "That lady should have at least let Sundae and Fudge give agility training a try."

Mom came and stood in her doorframe. "You sure you don't want me to walk with you?"

Robyn wanted to say, "Of course I want you to walk with me to school! I *need* you to walk with me!"

But she thought of her rules. What if no other parents of fifth graders were there? Everyone would think she was a baby. People are judgers (rule two).

Robyn scowled and yanked her shoelaces tight. "I'm old enough to go alone."

So she did, and her discomfort transformed once more. This time her mouth grew dry, and all the moisture that was supposed to surround her tongue sweated up her palms.

She passed the threshold onto the campus and tightened the straps on her backpack. A man with wire-framed glasses and a clipboard seemed to read the uncertainty in her eyes and asked her if she needed help.

But she knew her teacher's name—Mrs. Wang—and she knew her teacher's room number. So she rubbed her wet hands against her pants, made her way to her classroom, and stepped inside.

Cheery posters hung from the walls, and the desks

were arranged in pods of three or four. Each desk had a tent card with a name on it. She found the one that said ROBYN KELLEN and sat down.

Two other girls were already sitting across from her. One had a tent card that said LULU KARAMYAN. The other had a tent card that said MARSHAN KING.

The girl with the Lulu tent card said, "Do you believe in miracles?" She had short, wispy white hair, pale—almost see-through—skin, and her voice was as lilting as her name.

Robyn did not even have to think about it to realize that nothing on her list of new-kid rules had prepared her for such a question. So she lifted and dropped her shoulders in a way that was both friendly and non-committal.

The girl with the Marshan tent card piped up. She was African American and wore braces with rainbow-colored bands. The braces maybe embarrassed her because she kept covering her mouth when she spoke. She said, "We believe in miracles. You know why?" She pointed her chin at Lulu. "Because we are best friends, and the teacher doesn't even know that, and she still sat us right next to each other. Isn't that the most amazing thing you've ever heard?"

Truthfully, it *was* pretty amazing, and so too was the fact that *all three of them* had last names that started with *K*. "What are the chances of that?" marveled Robyn.

"I know," said Marshan. "It's so wild. I mean wow."

"Wow is right," said Lulu.

Mrs. Wang called the class to order, and the rest of the morning passed with the usual get-to-know-you activities. They were invited to decorate their name cards. They played a name game. The teacher read a story. They did a math review, during which Robyn realized that this school had gotten much farther along with fractions than her last school. It was a little scary. This too might be something people judged her about. They might say, "Oh, you're bad at math," or "Oh, you must not be very smart." But she knew how to handle this kind of problem. She just wouldn't let anyone find out.

The fact was, she was feeling pretty good. No flutters. No squeezes. All the moisture in her body was back where it was supposed to be. And it was all because of Lulu and Marshan. With that one conversation they had put her so much at ease. Was it possible? Could it be? Was the real miracle that Robyn had been seated next to two genuinely nice kids?

Halfway through the fraction review, Lulu whispered, "I see you-know-who is dressing all in *p-u-r-p-l-e* again this year."

Instinctively, Robyn looked around the room. Her eyes landed on a freckly girl with wavy brown hair. She wore a purple dress, a purple beaded necklace, and a bunch of purple barrettes.

"I saw that," whispered back Marshan. "I didn't even know she was in fifth grade."

Lulu leaned forward so that Robyn could hear too. "That's because she was in third grade last year. I know because she was in my sister's class. She must be skipping fourth grade."

"Wow," said Marshan, impressed. "She must be really smart."

"I know," said Lulu. She looked knowingly from Marshan to Robyn, and maybe she sensed how clueless Robyn felt because she said, "You know who we mean, right? Alejandra?" She made a pair of air quotes. "Aka the Grape."

Robyn confessed that she had only just moved to San Luis Obispo and didn't know anyone, let alone the girl in purple.

Both girls fell back in their chairs, their eyes growing round.

"I didn't know you were new," said Marshan, dropping her hand from her mouth and giving Robyn a welcoming smile.

"Me neither," said Lulu. Her expression grew concerned. "It must be hard to be new. Is it hard? Are you sad? Or scared?"

Robyn laughed, her body relaxing in response to their thoughtfulness. "I'm not sad or scared."

When they didn't seem to believe her, she tossed her long dark hair. "I've moved lots of times. I'm used to it."

"Oh, good," purred Lulu.

"Yeah, that's good. But if you are sad, you can tell us. We'll listen," added Marshan, a sympathetic tilt weighing her head to one side.

Robyn's heart began to swell. She almost believed that these girls were trying to befriend her. Right on the first day of school. But then she remembered rule number eight: Don't rush things. She flashed back to all the faces of all the people she'd buddied up to in the first weeks of past schools. Boy, had those efforts ended poorly. If there is one thing kids can smell, it is the desperation of the friendless.

The flutter returned to her belly. *Don't think these girls are your best friends just because they're being nice to you*, she told herself. *Play it cool. Take your time. Be patient.*

The teacher said it was time for another icebreaker. It was called Book Bingo, and they needed to go around the room and find people who had read the books on their Book Bingo card.

As Mrs. Wang began to pass out the cards, Marshan reached her hand toward Robyn. She said, "I should warn you. Don't call Alejandra Grape. She gets really mad when people do that."

"I wouldn't do that," said Robyn. Calling people names was looking for trouble (strictly forbidden by rule five). And it was mean. She'd been called enough names to know.

"I figured," said Marshan, sitting back. "But I just wanted to warn you. Alejandra can be a real Bradford pear tree."

Lulu knocked her elbow against Marshan's. Revealing a teacherly side that Robyn appreciated, she said, "Robyn doesn't know what that means. She wasn't here when we did that big tree project last year."

Smiling at Robyn, she said, "A Bradford pear tree has really brittle branches. They break off all the time. In snow. In wind. All the time."

Marshan added, "Alejandra breaks all the time too. She makes everything a big deal." She shrugged and shook her head. "It's better to be a coast live oak than a Bradford pear."

Lulu nodded. "Coast live oaks are very bendy in the windy. And they are native to the Central Coast of California."

Bendy in the windy. It made Robyn think of rule number ten: Be flexible. That was one of the most important new-kid rules of all. A new kid who couldn't be flexible was a new kid doomed to suffering.

She looked again at Alejandra. She seemed to be in a spat with the boy next to her. Her hand flew into the air, and she called, "Teacher!"

Mrs. Wang came over. One of her forearms was full of bracelets, and they all began to jangle as she crossed her arms to listen.

Alejandra spoke quickly, flailing her arms left and right. The boy, who had shoulder-length blond hair and blue eyes that somehow reminded Robyn of a snake, looked straight ahead, his fists tight. Robyn did not know what was going on, but she had a feeling that Alejandra was not being bendy in the windy.

She had heard and seen enough. Alejandra would need to be avoided. She was radioactive, and radioactive kids had the power to make other kids radioactive too. Robyn had fallen prey to their kind before. In Boulder, she made the mistake of hanging out with a wiggly and squirmy stinker. Not two weeks went by before the teacher assumed Robyn was a wiggly and squirmy stinker too. That had been a hard year. But it hadn't stopped Robyn from befriending a prickly tattletale in Portland who enjoyed handball just as much as her. But what difference did a shared interest have when everyone assumed that Robyn couldn't be trusted because, by mere association, she must be a prickly tattletale as well?

Enough was enough. She was never making that mistake again. Now she had her rules. And her rules would not steer her wrong. She would not look for trouble by spending time with someone like Alejandra. Because if she did that, people would judge her. And if they judged her, she wouldn't blend in, and if she couldn't blend in, it would be very hard to laugh things off. And if she couldn't laugh things off, someone might hurt her, and if they hurt her, it might be even harder not to let it show.

Day one. Lesson learned. Thank you, Lulu and Marshan. No Alejandra. No Alejandra ever.

CHAPTER 4

WITH THE EXCEPTION OF those pesky fractions, Robyn was doing pretty well by the end of her first week in San Luis Obispo. Her rules were not letting her down. They helped her laugh it off when the blond boy made eye contact from across the room and yelled, "What are you looking at?" They helped her keep a wide arc away from Alejandra, and when Lulu and Marshan asked about the places she'd lived and if she missed her friends, they kept her from glomming onto them like a burnt and goopy marshmallow.

But now it was lunchtime, the most dangerous hour of the day. Anything could—and probably would—happen. She could fall from the climbing structure, break an arm, and look up to find everyone gawking at her (Indianapolis). She could rip her pants open and be scarred for life (Chicago). Bullies might decide to target her for any old reason at all

(Boulder). Lunch recess was survival of the fittest. Lunch recess was eat or be eaten. Lunch recess was another reason she needed her rules. Rules like that? They were a tiny slice of order in a world of chaos.

She ticked her rules off on her fingers and considered her options.

She saw something that filled her with hope: for the first time, the playground assistant had brought out a ball for the handball wall. As new-kid rule number one plainly stated, the key to surviving as a new kid was blending in. The kid mistaken for a potted plant was the kid who survived to see another day. But if one had to be noticed, the place to be noticed was the sports field. Everyone loved an athlete. Being an athlete was, in and of itself, a Get-Out-of-Social-Weirdness-Free card. And while Robyn wouldn't normally consider herself athletic, she did consider herself the Queen of Handball. Because every school had a handball wall, and she had become an expert at knocking a ball against it. Was it a bold move to go over there so early in the school year? Probably. But handball was the one place she didn't mind sticking out.

Pushing back her shoulders, she walked confidently to the court and took her place at the end of the line. One by one, the players ahead of her took their turns, each silently accepting the universal rule that the winner played until the winner lost. But none of these winners were really all that great. So down went one winner, and, a few minutes later, down went another. Until it was Robyn's turn.

She got a good look at the current victor. It was Alejandra. She was dressed again in purple: purple shirt, purple leggings, purple socks, purple shoes.

Alejandra smiled a gap-toothed smile at Robyn. The gesture might have reassured a kid who didn't know anything about Alejandra, but Robyn had been warned. She could see the smile for what it was: trouble.

"I'm Alejandra," said the girl, bouncing the ball. "You're in my class."

Robyn knew that a radioactive kid couldn't make anyone else radioactive just by playing handball with them. The universal rule of handball assured that. It meant you weren't playing your friends or even anyone you particularly chose. You were just playing the next kid in line. So Robyn walked up to Alejandra and let the game begin.

Alejandra hit the ball against the handball wall. She said, "Are you new here?"

Robyn glanced at Alejandra before hitting the ball herself. "How did you know?"

The ball bounced close to the wall and Alejandra ran up to hit it. "Just guessed. I'm new too. Well, sort of, but my dad says I shouldn't talk about it. He says it's something people can be judgey about."

Robyn nodded, remembering rule number two: People are judgers. She willed Alejandra to listen to her dad.

"But you seem nice," said Alejandra, running back from the wall and getting to the ball just before it could take a second bounce. "The reason I'm only sort of new is because I've always gone to this school, but I just skipped fourth grade, and I don't really know any of the fifth graders."

There it was. Lulu and Marshan had been right. Alejandra had skipped fourth grade. It was proof that everything else they said was probably true too.

Robyn jumped sideways and slammed the ball back toward Alejandra.

Alejandra hit it easily. "But lots of fifth graders might already know that I skipped a grade because I won the Central California Coast Spelling Bee last year. I was the only third grader. It was on the news."

Robyn's fist landed on the side of the ball, which sent it spinning in an unexpected direction.

Alejandra jumped one way and then another, returning it right before it bounced once more. "Except now I remember that I'm not really supposed to talk about that either because my dad says people might think it sounds braggy, but I wasn't trying to be braggy. I'm just . . . it's hard to feel like you don't know anyone, especially when it seems like maybe everyone else already knows you. Or they think they know you when they really don't."

Robyn stopped. She stopped right there in the handball court and looked at Alejandra, stunned. Because Alejandra was right, she was exactly right. That *was* the constant new-kid challenge. You knew no one. But everyone *thought* they knew you. They knew you were the new kid, and that was all they saw you as until you showed them otherwise. But one slipup— one too-smelly lunch from home, one spill onto the ground, or overly loud guffaw, or bad joke about why the chicken crossed the road in a room where someone's pet chicken just got hit by a car, and that was it: the law of cause and effect. That was who you became in the eyes of others. It was like everyone else was a whole book, and you were just that one chapter.

And Robyn had been so many chapters. In Boulder, a representative of Guide Dogs of America had visited Robyn's school with her dog, Simba. The woman told them how the organization bred and trained Labrador retrievers to help the visually impaired and how only half of the dogs born into the program would ultimately have what it took to become a guide dog. Robyn had never heard a better and more fascinating speaker in her life. She asked question after question, and when the Q&A was over, she raised her hand and told the woman how Fudge was deaf and mostly blind and how Sundae was sort of like Fudge's own guide dog.

The woman had been so friendly, so supportive.

But when they returned to class, Robyn's teacher criticized her for talking too much. He did it right in front of her classmates too, and some of them snickered and laughed and called her a blabbermouth. But Robyn learned her lesson. She never asked or answered a single question in class for the rest of the year.

And that was nothing compared to Portland. The kids in her Portland school had the high-class humor of a polished toilet. One day, in a tumbling unit for PE, her sweaty T-shirt rolled up her back and her skin got suctioned up by the mat beneath her. The moment she moved, the suction released, producing a loud smacking noise. A boy named Garrett insisted she had farted. She denied it, but no one believed her. Why should they believe her? She was an unknown. She was the chapter titled "Farting Girl," or "Smellin' Kellen," because that was how she earned that charming and very durable name.

That was also how she scared off the entire fourth-grade class. She had gotten so embarrassed and mad that, one day at recess, she exploded at Garrett, saying a ton of things she didn't mean. His ears didn't line up. His breath smelled like hot dogs. He was so dumb that he thought eight plus eight equaled second helpings at dinner. Things like that.

People had laughed. Oh, boy had they laughed. They thought she was hysterical. So funny. So quick with the jokes.

But then they kept their distance. Because she'd become *that* chapter, the one called "Mean Under Pressure." And since no one knew when she might turn her mean-under-pressure tongue on them, they all treated her like a ticking bomb. Still, it had taught her the cause and effect of rule three: Fight fire with fire. A total pushover—a person who accepts a nickname like Smellin' Kellen—will get pushed again and again and again, and you don't want that. But, at the same time, don't burn down the whole school. Don't be a ticking bomb. No one likes a ticking bomb.

And now here she was, a new start in a new school, standing next to this grade-skipping, socially radioactive girl, who seemed to understand, who seemed to get the fact that being a new kid was being an impression, not a person. It was like a door inched open between them.

A boy shouted at Robyn. "Mooove. Your turn is over."

Her skin prickled. She—the Queen of Handball—had been so distracted by Alejandra's comments that she'd lost the game. But she didn't even care. She knew that voice. She knew that particular way of pronouncing the word "move." She turned. And there he was: the shaggy-haired boy from the park.

Gone were all thoughts of Alejandra. She stepped away from the handball court and bit down on her thumbnail as she watched Alejandra play, and beat, the boy.

Robyn watched him start to walk away, and then all of a sudden she found herself going over to him. Truly, she must have been possessed. It was the only way to explain why she was doing something so obviously against her rules. She should have taken a few days, spied on him, stalked him, figured out what kind of kid he was. But seeing him had reminded her anew of that first-love feeling she'd felt in the park, and she had made a promise to Sundae and Fudge that she would figure this agility thing out. Because now she understood something. There wasn't anything first-loveish about it. It was old love. It was her love for Sundae and Fudge. They just meant so much to her. They were the best friends she'd ever had. They cheered her up when she was sad. They blanketed her in support, and love. They never forgot her when she left to see her dad. They always remembered that she existed and showed her that they'd missed her presence when she returned. They were true blue. They were the best. And agility training was something she could give to them just because it was fun, and just because they would like it, and just because they'd be together. And, also, yes. She would love it too. Of course she would love it too. Who wouldn't? But they would love it *together*. That was why it mattered. That was why she couldn't let it go. And that was why, when faced with an opportunity to at least learn a little more about it, she couldn't focus on her wise and very important rules.

She said to the boy, "You were at the agility-training class."

He looked at her warily, like she was a word with too many syllables to decode.

Another boy joined him, the latest victim of Alejandra's killer handball skills. He was taller and thinner than the boy from the park, but they had the same slightly upturned noses and caramel-colored skin. He extended his hand. "Jonathan Pedrano. Nestor's cousin and business manager. How you doin'?"

He had something of a shampoo model's slickness about him. It made him seem a little untrustworthy, so she wasn't sure if he was joking about shaking her hand. An awkward moment passed and she clasped the tips of his fingers and then let go.

She looked back at the first boy, who now had a name: Nestor. A plan began to hatch inside her. She hadn't even known this plan had existed. But it had.

It had been hiding deep in her soul, like an Easter egg, and now it was cracking open, pouring out sharp pieces of shell and snotlike blobbiness. She said, "You're that dog-training lady's assistant."

He mumbled, "Umm. I'm that lady's grandkid."

"Yeah, but you help her. You know all about agility training."

"He does know all about agility training," said Jonathan, puffing up his chest. "He's the youngest person ever to compete in the finals of a California Canine Club agility competition."

"Really?" said Robyn. She had never heard of the California Canine Club, but she was still impressed. "Then, since you know so much, you could convince your grandma to teach my dogs. Fudge may be deaf and mostly blind, and Sundae may get all stressed out when he's not with Fudge, but they're very smart. Wherever we live, they always find a way to break into the dog treats. I know they can do agility."

Nestor glanced at his cousin and frowned. He shrugged and muttered, "Grandma Z. said no."

Jonathan raised his palms. "Listen," he said as if it were obvious. "If Grandma Z. said no, the answer is no. She's one stubborn cucumber."

Robyn began to turn from side to side. "But . . . maybe then *you* could teach me and my dogs agility training." It was not ideal. A class full of adults would be so much better, so much less judgmental. But that Easter egg was all slippery yolk now, and all she wanted to do was give her dogs something nice for a change, something that wasn't just her leaving them for an hour, or a day, or a month.

Nestor mumbled something and shoved his hands in his pockets.

Jonathan scratched his chin. Then he caught Nestor's eye, raised his eyebrows, and lifted his palms.

Nestor responded by rolling his eyes and smacking his palm against his forehead.

"Just a minute," said Jonathan, grabbing Nestor's arm and dragging him a short distance away.

The cousins dropped their heads toward each other and spoke briefly. Then they ran back.

"Okay," said Jonathan slickly. "We are willing to consider your offer."

As some point, Alejandra had joined them. Robyn didn't know when, but now Alejandra was there, and she gasped and threw her hands over her mouth, whispering, "Exciting development."

"You'll teach me and my dogs?" said Robyn, delighted and surprised and a little bit terrified, because her rules were finally catching up to her, and she realized that she knew nothing about this boy and his cousin. Nothing. And she had just invited them into two of the most important relationships in her life.

Jonathan ran a hand through his thick, shiny hair. "But here's the thing. It's gonna cost you."

The sudden image of Sundae and Fudge jumping through a hoop pushed away her reservations. "How much?" Mom paid for lots of classes. Surely, when Robyn explained that this was the grandkid of the dog-training lady, she would pay for this.

"Not money," said Nestor, sounding insulted.

Jonathan frowned. "We don't want money." He glanced around, as if he were worried that someone might be listening in. "We want math tutoring. You any good at math?"

"Absolutely, I'm . . ." Her voice trailed off as she thought about the fraction worksheets she'd been struggling with. "What exactly do you need help with?"

Too late. Nestor and Jonathan had seen the look on her face. They both sighed and slumped down.

"That's too bad," said Jonathan. "That would have been a good exchange of services."

But having pushed away her reservations, she was all in now. "If I paid you money, you could pay for a real tutor."

Jonathan shook his head. "We said no money. What do you want to do? Embarrass Nestor's parents? Make them think they can't afford a tutor for their own son? Think it through, girl-whose-name-I-don't-even-know."

"It's Robyn," said Robyn. "And I don't want to embarrass anyone. I'm just . . . not the best at fractions. *Yet.* But I could help you with—"

Jonathan squared his shoulders. "It's only fractions we need help with."

Alejandra cleared her throat. Speaking quickly, nervously, she said, "I'm good at fractions. I'm so good at fractions that I got to skip a whole grade." She paused a beat before adding, "That's not bragging. That's just the truth."

Jonathan and Nestor shared a glance. Then Jonathan's eyes narrowed. "Do you want Nestor to train *your* dog?"

"I don't have a dog," said Alejandra. "But I have seen agility training online, and I happen to think it is the best sport in the world."

She stood a little straighter and, with more confidence, said, "So I think I want in on this action. Here's what I'm thinking." She pointed to Robyn. "You bring the dogs." She pointed to Nestor. "You bring the agility training." She pointed to herself. "And I'll bring the math tutoring."

A dizzying wave coursed through Robyn. Everything was moving so fast! Too fast. She wasn't even entirely sure what was happening, but she did know that she had to hold on before it all slipped away.

Jonathan pointed at Robyn. "Doesn't seem like she's

bringing much. She'd get everything and do nothing."

No, no, no. That wouldn't do. She couldn't let Jonathan disrespect her like that. She was so close now. So. Very. Close. She dug in. "I'd be doing as much as you. What are you bringing to the table?"

He laughed. "I'd be doing way more than you. I'm Nestor's business manager. Exchanging dog training for math tutoring was my idea."

Robyn threw her hands in the air. "What kind of kid has a business manager?" She pointed a finger at him. "How about this? I bring the snack."

Jonathan steepled his fingers under his chin. "Yes," he said thoughtfully. "The snack. The *snack*. We have a deal."

Just then, the snake-eyed boy and one of his friends ran by and yelled, "Grape!"

Alejandra was after him in a flash, yelling, "That's not okay, Harrison. Harrison! Harrison! I'm telling Mrs. Wang."

The blond boy, Harrison, kept running, screaming, "Grape! Grape! Watch out! The Grape is on the move."

And then it hit Robyn: Alejandra. The breakable girl. The radioactive Bradford pear tree. Their—her— new math tutor.

Under her breath, she whispered, "Oh . . . maybe I just made a big mistake."

CHAPTER 5

FACT: ROBYN COULD HAVE backed out of the agility-training/math-tutoring/snack-supplying exchange. She thought about it. Repeatedly. But every time that happened, she'd think of Sundae and Fudge, and her longing to give them—and herself—the experience of learning that fun obstacle course would return, stronger than before.

But it was a whiplash sort of feeling—first wanting one thing, then wanting another—and she was having a hard time living with its confusing push and pull. Then it occurred to her that—duh—maybe this was the exact time to double-check her rules. Maybe there was something in them that would help her, something she wasn't remembering. And, sure enough, rule number seven to the rescue: Be nice to everyone.

She didn't need to let a little bit of social radioactivity keep her from doing something with Alejandra. She could simply be nice to Alejandra, just not so nice that she let Alejandra's radioactivity wear off on her. It was nothing personal. It was just survival.

That made everything so much easier. The next day, when Nestor handed Robyn a piece of paper and said, "Your dogs are going to need this kind of harness. They're also going to need treats," she took the paper and saluted him.

His expression grew grim. Urgently, he said, "Listen to me. The treats are the most important part. Get real chicken. Or maybe hot dogs. But watch the salt."

She covered all her bases. She made Mom buy low-sodium chicken hot dogs.

Truth be told, Mom was being a good sport about the class. She could have squashed everything. She could have said, "No way. The kid's grandmother said no. I said no. No means no." But she was being pretty open-minded about things.

As Robyn explained the deal she'd made with Nestor, Jonathan, and Alejandra, Mom strummed her fingers against the table. Then she said, "I would want—what's his name, Nestor?—to clear things with his grandmother."

Robyn didn't see that Nestor's grandmother had anything to do with anything. She wasn't part of the deal. Nestor, Jonathan, and Alejandra were. But she didn't want to get buried in technicalities with Mom either. She said, "Oh, she said it was fine. He talked it all over with her."

"Well, I guess it's okay then. But you better make it a good snack."

Robyn did. She got Milanos *and* Mint Milanos. She wanted everyone to get the message: her contribution was as valuable as anyone's. Added bonus. Sort of. She got to make another contribution. She got to deliver the grade-skipping math tutor. Robyn found out on the morning of the first class. Over breakfast, Mom explained that Alejandra's dad had found her number in the school directory and called. He had some complicated daycare issues and was wondering if Mom might be able to help him out. Well, no one appreciated complicated daycare scenarios more than Mom. Right away, she said that Alejandra could walk with Robyn and Nivien.

Robyn, who had been expecting to walk to Nestor's with just her dogs, balked. She wasn't sure what bothered her more, walking with Alejandra, which might increase the chances of Alejandra's radioactivity wearing off on her, or walking with Nivien—with really any babysitter—which would totally make Robyn seem like a little kid.

But as soon as she started to say anything, Mom gave her such a withering look that she zipped right up, lest Mom shut down the whole thing.

And this much was true: at least Alejandra made it easy, taking all the conversational burden off Robyn as she talked . . . and talked . . . and talked. The main object of her observations was a kid named William, a sixth grader she knew at the middle school. "William has a three-legged pit bull named Tiger. I don't know what happened to the fourth leg," Alejandra told Robyn. "I know William from my Argentine school." She stopped for a second and looked at Robyn.

Robyn and Nivien stopped too.

"You know what Argentine school is, right?"

Robyn shook her head.

Nivien said nothing, which was a little unusual for her. She wasn't the super-chatty type, but if something needed to be said, she said it. If Robyn tried to rush through her homework, Nivien would say, "Slow down." If Robyn tried to "forget" to take out the garbage or empty the dishwasher, Nivien would say, "I know you know that you need to do your chores." So when Alejandra expected them to know about Argentine school, Robyn thought for sure that Nivien would say something like, "How in the world would we know what that is?" But she didn't. She just let the question hang there.

No worries. Alejandra was not about to leave them in suspense. They started walking again, Alejandra explaining that Argentine school was where she went every Saturday to learn Spanish and Argentine culture.

She started to laugh. "The craziest things always happen to William in Argentine school. Twice, he slipped and fell into a pie. A real pie! Twice!"

Abruptly, she changed the subject. "I didn't say anything before because I didn't want to sound all obsessed or anything, but I'm obsessed with Nestor. That's one of the main reasons I wanted to do this, although I wasn't lying either. I have seen agility-training videos online, and I do think it is the coolest sport in the world."

Nivien snorted but kept her mouth closed and her eyes straight ahead.

"Umm," said Robyn. "Why are you obsessed with Nestor?"

Alejandra jumped high, kicking her heels against her bottom. "Because he's awesome. He's all, 'Grrrr. No one better mess with me. I'm Nestor.' He saved a baby from a shark."

Robyn did a double take. "No way."

"Yes way. He saved a real baby from a real shark. Everyone knows." She let out a squeal. "This is going to be so great."

Up ahead, they noticed a house decked out early for Halloween. There were ghosts, ghouls, mummies, and creepy clowns peeking out from behind trees, fake tombstones, and windows.

"I love it so much," said a breathless Alejandra.

Robyn had been following the directions to Nestor's house on her phone. She looked down at it and then back at the house. "I think that's where Nestor lives. Huh." She hadn't taken him for someone who went all out for holidays.

Alejandra began to run to the house.

Sundae and Fudge had been walking calmly this whole time, but now they seemed to sense that something exciting was about to happen. They barked at Alejandra's retreating figure and pulled on their leashes.

Robyn turned to Nivien. "Umm. I've got it from here." Then she and the dogs ran to the house.

A life-size skeleton wrapped in a black cloak stood on the doorstep. It had red eyes. It also turned out to have a motion detector. As soon as they got near it, a recorded voice let out an evil laugh and said, "We've been waiting for you."

Robyn and Alejandra screamed and then laughed as the door to the house next door swung open. Nestor and Jonathan came running out.

Nestor loud-whispered, "Shhhhhhhh! You'll set them off!"

From inside the house with the skeleton came a frantic, deep-throated barking. An enormous midnight-colored poodle whipped aside the curtain. Immediately, it was joined by two slightly less-enormous midnight-colored poodles. They had teeth the size of fingers and more spit than . . . well, they had a *lot* of spit. The big one had eyes as red as the skeleton's. But that turned out to be a trick of the reflection.

"You went to the wrong house," complained Nestor. "You went to my grandparents'. My house is next door."

"Now these dogs will never shut up," sighed Jonathan. He pointed his finger at the biggest dog. "Yeah, I'm looking at you, Bruce."

The barking got quieter, but only because the biggest dog was now growling.

Robyn was only half paying attention to any of this. She hadn't realized it at first, but the skeleton had rattled Sundae, and now the roaring sound of the poodles was making it worse. His tail was tucked between his legs, and he was shaking as he tried to climb on top of Fudge. Robyn bent down to comfort him.

"Sorry. I guess I read the address wrong," said Robyn, lifting him off Fudge and running her hand down his back.

"You definitely read the address wrong," said Jonathan.

She murmured to Sundae that everything was okay. Then she said to Nestor, "Your grandma really likes Halloween."

"If Grandma Z. does something," said Jonathan, "she does it all the way."

"I brought two kinds of cookies," Robyn said, glancing over at Nivien.

Nivien stood where she was and was watching them, but, catching Robyn's eye, she winked and mouthed, "One hour." That was when she'd be back.

Robyn nodded and stood back up just as Jonathan said, "Oh, we're gonna have to see those cookies."

She took them out of her backpack and gave them to him.

Ignoring the still-barking poodles, the two cousins brought Robyn and the suddenly quiet and blushing Alejandra over to Nestor's back gate. It was locked, which Robyn didn't think too much about until Jonathan explained that it was a necessary precaution. At one point, the gate had only had a latch, but the poodles had figured out how to undo it. Soon afterward, they'd gone after the postal carrier. Now both Zazueta families had to pick up their mail at the post office.

Nestor unlocked the gate and ushered them inside.

Robyn's jaw dropped.

Jonathan was right: when Mrs. Zazueta did things, she really did them.

The two Zazueta households had combined their backyards into one large space, and Nestor's grandmother must have overseen all of it, because the whole thing had been transformed into one enormous, magnificent agility course. It had hurdles, tire swings, balance beams, seesaws, and other pieces of agility equipment that Robyn didn't recognize, including two tall boards angled together at the top like a steep roof, and a set of square tables, nested one under the other. Mixed in with everything were dirty tennis balls and rope toys that glistened with dried drool.

Noses twitching, Sundae and Fudge pulled on the ends of their leashes. At Nestor's suggestion, Robyn unleashed them so they could sniff around.

A scratching sound erupted near Mrs. Zazueta's house.

Robyn turned to see the poodles clawing at a sliding glass door. Their mouths were open, and their breath was beginning to steam up the glass.

"Don't worry. That glass is thick," said Jonathan. He'd opened the bag of Milanos and munched on one. He looked over at the poodles. "You hear that, Bruce? You're never getting through that glass."

Alejandra finally found her voice. She said, "Why don't you like Bruce?"

Jonathan stared at the window. "He knows."

Another figure walked into view and lined up next to the poodles. He had a thick white mustache. Everything about him was rectangular. His head. His torso.

He could have been made of LEGO pieces. He nodded at them.

Nestor and Jonathan waved.

"That's Grandpa Z.," said Jonathan, who kept waving until the old man shuffled away from the glass.

"By the way," said Jonathan casually. "Um . . . there is one little thing we should mention. I wouldn't even have remembered it if I hadn't seen Grandpa Z., but . . . Grandpa Z., of course, knows about our exchange. We told him because he babysits us and stuff, but . . . nobody else needs to know about this."

"My dad knows," said Alejandra quickly. "And everyone in Argentine school. And Mrs. Wang. And the lunch assistant at school. And my swimming teacher."

Jonathan waved a hand. "They're okay. I mean, if you happen to run into Nestor's grandma or his mom and dad . . . maybe you don't need to tell them. Okay?"

"I don't even know who they are," said Alejandra.

"Which is why you should be all *shhhhhh* about the whole thing. Because you wouldn't even know if you were talking to them."

Robyn knew a good sneakaroo when she heard one. She didn't know why Nestor and Jonathan were keeping the lessons secret from Nestor's grandma and parents, but they were. And she knew the universal rule about sneakaroos: What you don't know can't hurt you. She gave a curt nod and kept her mouth closed.

But Alejandra did not know the universal rule of sneakaroos. She said, "Why?"

Jonathan's voice, always so smooth, broke. "No, uh . . . no reason." He motioned to the agility equipment and smiled slyly. "Wanna do people agility?"

"Yes!" hollered Alejandra.

Robyn was about to say the same thing when Nestor grunted, "We're not supposed to." He was setting up shop on a small patio behind his own house, one of the only parts of the yard that did not look like it had been designed for playful dogs. His backpack lay on a large outdoor dining table, and he pulled out his math book.

Jonathan shrugged, explaining, "We broke the A-frame last time."

"The A-frame?" said Robyn.

Jonathan pointed at the roof-shaped device. "The dogs have to climb up and down it."

"*And,*" mumbled Nestor, "they have to hit the contact zone."

The contact zone. It was their first agility lesson. Some obstacles had contact zones, areas the dogs had to touch with all four paws. Agility wasn't just about speed. It was about precision.

Robyn looked around one more time, her eyes landing, inevitably, on the curly-furred poodles, who still stood staring from the window. The two less-enormous poodles were mostly settled, but Bruce's eyes were wide. His mouth twitched. His teeth glistened.

"Where's the big white dog?" she asked.

"You mean Gigante," said Jonathan.

"He's with Grandma at one of her classes," said Nestor.

He explained that Mrs. Zazueta took Gigante everywhere she could. Gigante was the perfect dog—a walking advertisement of Mrs. Zazueta's talents as a trainer. The poodles? They were works in progress, especially Bruce, who had an inner-ear condition that affected his balance. It made it so that he was always knocking things over and running into people.

At least that's what Nestor said.

Jonathan said Bruce was an evil genius who knew exactly what he was doing. But he also said that Bruce was one of the reasons they were all there. "Nestor has taught Bruce a little agility. We figure if he can teach *Bruce*, he'll definitely be able to teach your dogs."

A loud thud on the picnic table caused Robyn, Jonathan, and Alejandra to turn their heads. Nestor had dropped his math book on the table and was shaming them with an impatient frown.

"Okay!" said Alejandra. "Let's get our math on." She was a little fidgety, and she kept glancing at Nestor, smiling, and then looking away.

They all pulled out their homework and soon got

to a word problem about too many kids and too few pizzas.

"Why is it always pizzas?" moaned Jonathan.

For once, Robyn found herself in agreement with him. "Yeah," she said. "So many problems would be solved if people just didn't skimp on the pizzas."

Alejandra and Jonathan laughed, and even Nestor chuckled.

A weight lifted off Robyn, one she didn't even know was there.

And Alejandra was true to her word. She walked them through the problem—and the rest of the homework—like she'd been helping people with math her whole life.

"Dang, Alejandra," said Jonathan when they were done. "You're good at this stuff."

"Yeah," Nestor said, nodding. "Thanks."

Alejandra's cheeks began to turn pink. When the boys turned to repack their backpacks, she whispered to Robyn, "Nestor Zazueta said 'Thanks' to me."

Nestor told Robyn to releash Sundae and Fudge.

She felt a giddy thrill as she ran to the dogs and connected the leashes to their harnesses. "This is it, guys! Are you ready? Are you excited? You're gonna love it. I know you are."

Nestor rubbed his hands together. "Let's start with

something easy. The tire swing." He pointed to a large hoop that hung from the center of a wooden frame. The hoop looked a lot like a bicycle tire, which Nestor unnecessarily explained was why it was called a tire jump. The point, he said, was to get the dog to jump through the hoop.

He adjusted the swing so that the bottom of the tire rested on the ground.

Then he told Robyn what he wanted her to do. He said her job was to be the *dog handler* (agility lesson two: the person who directed the dog around the course was called the handler), and that all she needed to do was follow four simple steps.

1. Stand with the dogs at the front of the tire swing.
2. Remove the leashes and tell the dogs to stay.
3. Walk to the other side of the jump and call the dogs to her.
4. Shower Sundae and Fudge—who would naturally follow behind him—with praise and pieces of hot dogs when they came to her.

"And what do I do?" said Alejandra, excited.

Nestor crinkled his eyes. "Watch?"

"Oh." She sounded disappointed. "Okay."

"It's all right, Little A," said Jonathan, still sitting

at the outdoor table. He held up the Mint Milanos. "We're gonna finish these off. And then you can tell me the story of your life."

Perking up, Alejandra said, "Fun!" and she joined Jonathan at the table.

Robyn walked with the dogs to the front of the tire jump. This was it. The moment she had been waiting for, the moment that this love-at-first-sight passion would finally reveal its wonders. She stifled a happy squeal and unleashed the dogs. "Stay," she said firmly. Then she made her way to the other side of the device.

She turned around to find Fudge and Sundae inches from her feet. They had followed her the whole way.

Nestor mumbled, "You didn't say 'stay' right. You have to sound firm, but you also have to sound friendly and excited. Try it again."

They tried it again. And again.

Sometimes the dogs followed her. Sometimes they went back to the table and sniffed for crumbs. Sometimes they sat there, or wandered off somewhere else, or licked their fur.

Nestor grew grumpy. "I don't think your dogs know how to stay at all."

Robyn looked confused. "Isn't that what they're learning now?"

"No," said Nestor, an annoyed blast of air stretching out the word. "That's basic dog training. You didn't tell me your dogs didn't know the basics. They need to know those before they can do this."

She rested her hands on her hips. "You never said that. And they do know the basics. They know not to pee in the house."

He threw up his arms. "That's not the basics. That's the minimum. The basics were implied. Every person who has a dog should at least teach them the basics." He started counting off with his fingers. "Sit. Stay. Come. Leave it. Things like that."

She sucked in her breath. "Oh. Don't tell me what my dogs should know. They have a very tragic backstory. We've done our best. Besides, you're the teacher; you should have been more clear."

Alejandra joined them. "Hey . . . um . . . this reminds me of this time my friend William drove with his parents all the way to the natural history museum in Los Angeles to see this special exhibit on tiny dinosaurs, but when they got there, the museum was closed."

Nestor was looking at Alejandra. His eyes had grown very glossy.

Robyn said, "What?"

"Some water pipe burst or something. I don't remember. But . . . you know . . . no museum. And they'd driven all that way just for that. So they went to Hollywood instead. And there was a person dressed like Elmo, and William said he was skinny and grimy and creepy. He ended up having nightmares for days. William, not the Elmo. Although who knows. He could have been having nightmares too.

"But the good news was that William's parents did find a really good donut store. He brought us all donuts. In Argentine school."

There was a long moment of quiet.

Finally, Jonathan stood up. He nestled the cookie bag in the crook of his elbow and walked over. "The point is, you guys are being Elmos."

Alejandra shook her head. "No. The point is that sometimes you just don't know things, and it's no one's fault."

Jonathan nodded. "Yeah. That's a better point."

Nestor snorted. He looked at Robyn. "You're going to have to teach them to sit. They at least need to do that. You can look up how on YouTube."

She nodded. "Fine. Then you're gonna have to be nicer when I don't know things."

"Okay," he muttered into his neck. A moment later, he said, "Well, we're already here. Let's try this a different way."

He told Robyn to leash up the dogs and then hand the leashes to Jonathan and Alejandra, which she did.

"Now go to the other side of the tire swing and call Sundae," he said. Then he turned to Alejandra and Jonathan. "As soon as she calls him, let go of the leashes."

Perfection.

From the other side of the tire swing, Robyn called Sundae. Alejandra and Jonathan released the leashes. Whoosh! The dogs sailed through the tire.

Alejandra and Jonathan cheered as Robyn bent down to give the dogs their hot dogs.

"You did it," she said to Sundae and Fudge. "I knew you could. I'm so proud of you."

She stood up, a satisfied look on her face. "I told you they could do it."

Nestor grunted, but he looked pleased too.

They repeated the task until the dogs understood what to do. Then Nestor adjusted the tire jump so that the bottom of the tire was a few inches off the ground.

They tried the jump again.

Zoom! Sundae was at Robyn's side almost before she'd finished saying, "Tire!"

But Fudge was not.

She had tried. She had started following Sundae the moment he moved, but she hadn't seen the bottom of the tire until it was too late. She careened into it, falling forward onto her snout. She wasn't hurt; the tire was very light. She was shaken, though. She shook her head and dropped her tail between her legs. Then she sniffed the tire and backed away, not sure what to do next.

Without even waiting for his hot dog, Sundae ran back to her. He nuzzled Fudge's neck, and she shook her whole body and knocked her torso into his.

Robyn rushed over to Fudge and began to pet her, saying, "It's okay. It's okay."

She looked at Nestor. Everyone was looking at Nestor.

His arms were crossed, and he was tapping one foot. "Let's try it again."

They tried it again. This time Fudge tripped. One of her front legs stepped over the tire, but the other one collided into it. She sniffed again at the tire. Unsure what to do, she shook herself and got flustered all over again when the swaying tire swung back and tapped against her head.

The problem was that she was not jumping. She was barely jogging, and she was barely jogging because she didn't realize she had to jump, and she didn't realize she had to jump because of her poor vision.

"Okay," said Nestor. "We're done."

"So soon?" asked Alejandra. She was standing over Robyn, who was back trying to reassure Fudge.

"She's not having fun," said Nestor. "If we keep going, she could get more spooked."

"But . . ." Alejandra started twisting one of her long curls around her finger. "Maybe something else would be fun." She pointed to the A-frame.

"No," said Nestor. "That's it." There was something so final about the way he spoke. So permanent.

Robyn stood up. "But . . . we'll try again next week, right?"

The question hung over all of them, unanswered.

Finally, Nestor pointed at Fudge. "If she can't jump . . ."

Jonathan nodded. "Yeah. She has to be able to jump. There's lots of jumping in agility."

Nestor pointed an angry finger at Jonathan. "I just said that!"

Jonathan shrugged in apology. Waving a hand, he turned to Robyn and said, "Never mind. He just said that."

Robyn looked down again at sweet Fudge. She had shaken off her run-in with the tire and was sniffing at a bug. Sundae was trying to nose his way into Robyn's pocket so he could get at the hot dog pieces.

Robyn looked around the obstacle course as if seeing it for the first time. The tire swing. The hurdles. The balance beam—what was it—four feet off the ground? The A-frame? It had to be five feet high. And that seesaw. Would Fudge really be able to cross a constantly rebalancing seesaw just by following Sundae?

The device was probably only a foot wide.

Robyn sat on the ground. She hated to admit it, but she wondered if Mom and Mrs. Zazueta had been right after all. Maybe this was too dangerous for Sundae and Fudge.

Alejandra tilted her head one way and then another. "Well, who cares if the tire is on the ground or off the ground? Who cares if Fudge even does the tire? Just let Fudge do the things she wants to do. Let them both do the things they want to do, the way they want to do them."

Nestor was shaking his head. "No. Agility has rules."

Jonathan said, "Yeah. Agility is all about rules."

Nestor once again pointed an angry finger at Jonathan.

This time, Jonathan lifted his palms. In his best shampoo-model voice, he added, "But it doesn't have to be about rules. Does it?"

"Exactly," said Alejandra. "Rules are overrated. You should just have fun."

A lump hardened in Robyn's throat. Rules were not overrated. Rules were the difference between chaos and order, safety and danger. But . . . in this case, did they have to be?

Robyn looked at Nestor. His arms were crossed, and his lips were pencil-thin, as if he were thinking the same thing.

Jonathan added, "And Alejandra is a good math tutor."

Nestor nodded, admitting, "She is a good tutor." He looked up. "Come back next week. Let me think on it."

CHAPTER 6

ROBYN WILLED HERSELF TO believe that the youngest boy ever to compete in the finals of a California Canine Club agility contest—a boy who could teach agility to a wild, evil-genius, balance-challenged poodle—would find a way to make the agility lessons work for Sundae and Fudge. So she did what she was supposed to. She spent the next week figuring out how to teach Sundae and Fudge to sit on command. Nestor had been right. There were tons of videos on YouTube. And the steps they recommended weren't that hard. Like agility training, they were built around getting dogs to exchange actions for treats. And how could dog handlers signal the action they wanted? With hand signals and verbal commands.

That was fine for Sundae. Ever eager for food, he learned the sit command quickly.

The problem was Fudge. She couldn't hear verbal commands. She couldn't see hand signals. But Robyn couldn't believe those were the only choices. For two nights after dinner, she sat on the couch, pulled out her phone, and Googled her options.

The first time Mom saw her, she said, "Hey, this is our together time. No phones. The couch is now a no-phone zone."

When Robyn explained what she was doing, Mom pulled out her own phone and joined in the search.

Then Robyn found it: a website all about teaching hearing- and visually impaired dogs by using touch commands. For sit, it recommended using two taps on the rump. There was even a video.

She showed the video to Mom.

"So let's do it," Mom said, heading straight to the kitchen to cut up some hot dogs.

Robyn took a piece and held it about a foot above Fudge's nose. Fudge instantly lifted her head toward the scent. Then Robyn stepped a little closer so that Fudge had to sit and lengthen her neck to stay near the reward. As soon as Fudge sat, Robyn gave her two taps on her bottom and a treat.

Fudge was no fool. She quickly figured out that two taps meant sit, and sit meant treat. By the end of the training session, she was bumping her butt into Robyn, hoping that would count as a tap.

"I have to admit," said Mom, "I was dubious."

"I knew you were," said Robyn, a proud, but also a

little smug, smile pulling up her lips. "But I wasn't."

"No, you were not," said Mom. "You were right."

"I *was* right. You know why? Because our dogs are as good as anyone's dogs."

"You better believe it," said Mom.

"Oh, you better," said Robyn.

Sundae came and bumped Fudge out of the way. He looked hard at Robyn. He wanted training treats too. So she switched back to the voice and hand commands, and Fudge jumped on the couch and rolled onto her belly, eager for Mom to give her a belly rub.

A smile planted itself on Robyn's mouth, and it stayed there until the next morning, when she went to school. Nestor might have been a dog-training pro, but she'd found the touch-training website, and she couldn't wait to tell him about it. She saw him and Jonathan as they were entering the campus. She ran up to them and pulled out her phone. "You've got to see this!"

Strictly speaking, the school was a no-phone zone too. And teachers were much more serious about not seeing phones than Mom. So Robyn, Nestor, and Jonathan looked sneakily about as she pulled out her phone and found the website.

They looked up at the sound of approaching footsteps. Alejandra was running toward them. "Hey, is that a pho—"

"SHHHH!"

They made space for her in their huddle, and Robyn showed the video of a blind and deaf dog learning the sit command.

"Touch commands," muttered Nestor. "I should have thought of that."

"I tried it last night and it worked perfectly," Robyn explained. "I'll work with Sundae and Fudge all week. They'll for sure be ready to go for our next lesson."

Nestor, Jonathan, and Alejandra smiled their approval.

And, for a moment, those smiles were all Robyn needed. It was like when she'd met Lulu and Marshan, but it was different too. On that first day of school, they'd been so sympathetic, so friendly. She'd felt *grateful* to Lulu and Marshan. She didn't feel like she owed her gratitude to Nestor, Jonathan, and Alejandra, though. Theirs was an exchange of services, after all, and the delivery of Milanos was a pretty valuable service. But she did feel like they were all a part of something. Something great. Something yet to come. It was . . . fun.

The bell rang and they ran to class.

She sat down to find Marshan and Lulu sighing and regarding her with deep concern.

"Harrison's being such a jerk," said Marshan.

Lulu knitted her brows together and leaned across

her desk. "We heard him talking to some people. He said he saw you talking not just to Alejandra, but also to Nestor Zazueta and Jonathan Pedrano. He said, 'Who does that new girl think she is?'"

Whatever Robyn had felt earlier with Alejandra, Nestor, and Jonathan disappeared, replaced by a lump in her throat.

Marshan leaned even farther over her own desk. "This boy Marcus said that maybe you were a grape too."

"But I don't even wear purple," said Robyn, who knew as soon as she said it that sometimes a grape is more than a color, or even a fruit. Sometimes a grape is something to be squished.

She flopped back in her chair and let out a soft moan. "It's just . . ." She explained the dog-training arrangement she'd made with Nestor, Jonathan, and Alejandra. "I was just telling them something I'd figured out. I didn't know . . ."

She dropped her head in her hands. How had she let herself be so stupid? In all her excitement about touch training, she'd forgotten about her rules. Again! Now she'd made herself a big old bull's-eye for Harrison. Harrison with the snake eyes. She knew his type. He was like the teacher who said she talked too much. He was like the kids who thought she was a prickly tattletale just because she was friends with someone who was a prickly tattletale. He was a judger. He was a judger who'd noticed her and who was looking to make trouble. She could feel it in her bones.

To make matters worse, now she was left wondering what Harrison had meant. Who did *he* think she thought she was? Was he only judging her for talking to Alejandra? If that was the case, why had he cared about her talking to Nestor and Jonathan? Was there something wrong with talking to Nestor and Jonathan? Were they radioactive too? They didn't seem radioactive.

Lulu reached out her hand and patted Robyn's fingers. "You can talk to us at lunch about how sad this makes you, if you want."

A lifeline! A way out! A way to get Harrison's snake eyes to move onto some other poor sucker by letting Robyn blend in with a pair of real blender-inners! A blossom of hope opened inside her.

"That would be nice," she said.

When lunch came, Lulu and Marshan ushered her to a table. It was like they were her bodyguards, with one on either side of her.

But Alejandra found her way to that table too.

It was so awkward. It was so bad. Robyn didn't want to be mean to Alejandra—she actually liked Alejandra—but the whole reason she was sitting with Marshan and Lulu was to get some distance from the radioactive girl, not to get sucked further into her orbit.

Alejandra tried to engage. "Sundae and Fudge are so cute, aren't they?"

"Hmmm?" said Robyn, not making eye contact even though Alejandra was directly across from her. "Oh, yeah," she said blandly. "For sure."

"Remember when you said they always find ways to break into their treats? How have they done that?"

This time Robyn pretended she couldn't even hear Alejandra. Instead, she started laughing, just because Lulu and Marshan were laughing, just so Alejandra would get the picture: they weren't really friends. They were just people who did an activity together.

When Robyn had finished eating, Alejandra nudged her. "Wanna play handball?"

"Oh . . . not today. I'm not really in the mood," Robyn said, guilt swimming inside her as a flash of understanding crossed Alejandra's face, a flash that said, "Oh. This girl is not really interested in me."

Alejandra lifted her chin. "Okay," she said softly before running off to the handball wall.

Be nice to everyone. Rule seven popped into her head, filling her with shame. But gosh if that wasn't the hardest rule of all. It seemed to counter so many of the other rules. If you're going to lay low and blend in, how can you be nice to everyone? If you're not going to let people judge you or let them know that they've hurt you, or if you're going to fight fire with fire, how can you possibly, always, be nice to everyone?

She rested her forehead in her hands and sighed.

Marshan turned to her. "Are you worried about Harrison? Don't be. He's a jerk."

"He always has been," said Lulu. "Even in first grade."

Robyn sat a little straighter. "What has he done?"

Lulu rolled her eyes. "What hasn't he done? I can't even remember them all."

"Well, thank you for letting me eat with you," said Robyn. She meant it too. She was still feeling glum about Alejandra, but not so glum that she didn't appreciate how much Lulu and Marshan were trying to help her.

"Are you mad?" asked Marshan. "I would be mad if I heard Harrison talking about me behind my back. I would be mad and sad. And maybe nervous because . . . what's he going to do?" Alarm splashed across her face. "Do you think he'll say something to you? What will you do if he says something?"

Robyn cocked her head and thought about it. She knew the problem wasn't so much what Harrison might say to her. She could handle that. It was more how he might, with very little effort, color other people's opinion of her. He already had, after all. Even now, people were looking at her differently. Even now, some boy named Marcus was wondering if she was a grape and others were wondering if she was as breakable as Alejandra.

She took a deep breath and tried to steel herself. "I don't know. But I've dealt with worse."

Lulu shook her head. Smacking her lips, she said, "What was the worst?"

Robyn looked from Lulu to Marshan. To share a sad story with people you didn't know well—no matter how nice they seemed—was not wise. Give people ammunition and they might be tempted to use it against you later. She shrugged and said, "When you're an experienced new kid like me, you try and put the past behind you."

"Wow," said Marshan. "That sounds very smart."

Robyn shrugged. "It's all about survival."

Lulu and Marshan nodded gravely.

"Survival," whispered Lulu.

"Yeah," said Marshan. "Survival."

CHAPTER 7

THE DAYS TICKED OFF. In the evenings, Robyn worked with Sundae and Fudge to perfect their sit. At school, she gently tried to untether herself from any encounters with Alejandra, but also with Nestor and Jonathan. Because what if Harrison *had* implied that they were radioactive too? She just didn't think she could risk it.

But it definitely made things weird. One time, the three of them ran up to her at afternoon recess.

Jonathan said, "Nestor wants to know how Sundae and Fudge are doing with their sit. Because he has some training ideas."

"Oh," she said, casually looking around to see if Harrison—or anyone—might be watching them. "They're doing great. I'll see you later."

Then she turned around and walked the other way. She'd been with Lulu and Marshan. She'd been hanging out with them ever since that day Harrison turned his cold-blooded gaze on her. The three of them had been walking around the blacktop, just doing nothing, just talking.

"Nestor sounds like a pretty serious dog trainer," said Lulu.

"Yeah," said Marshan. "Is he good?"

"For sure," said Robyn, shaking her hair as if she were shaking away the subject of Alejandra, Nestor, and Jonathan, as if anything having to do with them might jinx her. "So . . . what do you guys do for fun when you're not at school?"

Lulu pulled up her sleeve to show off two long scratches. "We like to dress up our cats," she said. Then she explained how she and Marshan used their large collections of American Girl doll clothes as cat costumes.

"Then we take pictures," said Marshan. "Sometimes our moms put them on Instagram."

"We also take a sewing class, because you can only get so creative with doll dresses."

Lulu asked if Robyn ever dressed her dogs in clothes.

Robyn laughed. "No. It would make Sundae too nervous, and Fudge would be too confused about what the heck was going on."

When they asked why, she explained about Fudge's disabilities.

"Poor Fudgey!" said Marshan, her fingers flying up to her face.

"What happened?" asked Lulu.

Robyn sighed. Then she shared Sundae and Fudge's tragic backstory, knowing full well that it would break their sensitive hearts, and that they would like that. It boiled down to this: a hoarder had managed to fill his rural Arizona home with over seventy Jack Russell terriers and Jack Russell terrier mixes. All of the dogs experienced one kind of trauma or another—from run-ins with coyotes, to 115-degree temperatures, to who knew what. That was why Sundae was so dependent upon Fudge and why Fudge—who had probably endured numerous untreated infections—had lost her hearing and most of her sight.

"But eventually some rescue group came in," said Robyn. "They split up the dogs and sent them to a bunch of other rescue places. We got Sundae and Fudge from one in Boulder. Since they were so bonded, the rescue group said we had to adopt them together. We were all, 'Of course. You can't be breaking up bonds all bing-bang-boop. That's traumatizing." She was quiet for a minute; then she added, "That's why I like that they're doing agility training. They deserve good things after all the bad things they've been through."

"That's the worst story I've ever heard in my life."

Lulu was shaking her head and wringing her hands. "Poor, poor Fudge."

"Poor, poor Fudge," said Marshan, her palms covering her mouth.

The bell rang and they began walking back to class.

Having expected their sympathy, Robyn wasn't surprised by all the "poor Fudges." But where were the "poor Sundaes"? He'd lived with the same neglectful owner as Fudge. And while it was true that he had not lost his sense of hearing or sight, in some ways, he had been scarred even more deeply. "Sundae's afraid of almost everything," she told them.

"Oh," they said, one after the other. "Poor Sundae."

"But it's still worse for Fudge," said Marshan.

"Yeah," said Lulu. "Poor little Fudge."

"Actually, being scared most of the time is pretty awful."

"Actually . . ." It was Alejandra. She had fallen in behind them, her face red and sweaty from handball. ". . . No one should feel sorry for Sundae and Fudge. They're brilliant."

"That's true," said Robyn, holding up a finger. "They're brilliant, and smart, and they have great senses of humor. They have this joke where they steal my mom's underwear and run around with it. She'll chase them all over the house. It's so funny. You can tell they're laughing with their tails."

Alejandra started to giggle, but she giggled a little too loudly and for a little too long.

Robyn saw Lulu and Marshan shoot each other a glance, and her stomach turned to ice when, in the distance, she saw Harrison become very still. He seemed to have heard something. Maybe Alejandra. Maybe her.

"Um," said Robyn, picking up her pace. "I forgot. I have to ask Mrs. Wang something. See ya."

That was it. For the rest of the afternoon, Robyn kept extra alert, making sure she wasn't getting any unwanted looks or smirks from Harrison. She didn't think she did. But it had been a close one, and she knew she would have to be even more careful about maintaining that boundary between who she was and who she talked to at school versus at Nestor's.

But that got a little trickier the next day. In class, each pod of desks had been given pieces of a paper skeleton. They were supposed to figure out how to assemble it and then guess what kind of animal it was supposed to be. Robyn was pretty convinced that her group was making a dog skeleton.

"You can tell by the shape of the head and the legs and the tail," she said.

"I don't know," said Lulu. "It could just as easily be a cat. It's too small to be a dog."

"But dogs can be small," said Robyn. "And look, it's got a snout."

Marshan sighed. "Pigs have snouts, not dogs, and it's definitely not a pig. I think Lulu's right. I think it's a cat."

Lulu nodded. "Yeah, it's for sure a cat."

"Um," said Robyn, who knew that it was definitely *not* a cat. "Well, maybe you're right."

"Okay. We'll write down 'cat' when we get to that part," said Lulu. She tilted her head and it seemed like she wanted to make it up to Robyn, for disagreeing with her. "But speaking of dogs, how is your class going for your poor little cutie dogs?"

And this was the tricky part. It would have been so much easier to not even have to bring it up, because bringing it up also meant bringing up Alejandra, Nestor, and Jonathan. Robyn tried to keep it short. "Our next class is today, so we'll see how it goes."

"Oh," cooed Marshan. "Sweet Fudgey. Things must be so hard for her."

"Hey," said Lulu. "Will you do us a favor? It's something we've been wondering. When you're with Alejandra, can you just ask her *why* she wears so much purple? Because . . . why?"

Robyn swallowed hard. This was the opposite of securing boundaries between the worlds of dog training and school. This was bringing the worlds of dog training and school closer together. Plus, Alejandra wouldn't like it, and Robyn had no interest in poking that particular bear. But Marshan and Lulu had been so nice to her, and somehow Robyn found herself saying, "Okay. I'll ask."

Yet, when it was finally time to do so, when they were finally walking to agility training—she couldn't do it. She looked at Alejandra in her purple skirt, purple tights, and purple top, and the words just wouldn't come.

She wished she could blame Nivien somehow. But Nivien was six feet back. She'd been giving the girls their space for the entire walk. Robyn doubted she could even hear them.

About a block from Nestor's, she finally mustered her courage. "Why do you like purple so much?" She could hear the impatience in her voice, but her tone wasn't *so* bad. She certainly didn't think she deserved the reaction she got from Alejandra, who spat, "I can wear whatever color I want."

Still walking, Robyn gave Alejandra a sideways glance. She could see that the younger girl's face had darkened, and her jaw was clenched. She could only think of one word: breakable. Alejandra was so breakable.

"It's not a big deal. It was just a question," said Robyn.

Fudge stopped to pee, and Robyn held back.

Alejandra faced her.

"I know people think it's weird. I'm not stupid."

Robyn pulled on the leash and started walking again. She tried hard to sound neutral. "I didn't say it was weird. I was just curious."

Alejandra blinked. Her mouth dropped open, and it suddenly looked like she was about to talk. Then her lips clamped shut, and she looked straight ahead. But by the time they reached Nestor's and they'd said goodbye to Nivien, she'd relaxed again.

Robyn had brought two snacks this time: slice-and-bake cookies that she'd made herself and a big bag of popcorn.

"Oh, I love me some slice-and-bake," said Jonathan, grabbing two.

Cookies and popcorn in hand, they gathered around the table to begin their math homework. It was more of the same: fractions, fractions, fractions, with some decimals thrown in for good measure.

Robyn looked at Sundae and Fudge. They were standing at Mrs. Zazueta's sliding glass door. Behind the glass sat the poodles, who were once more lined up all in a row. At the end stood Nestor's grandfather. Nestor had brought him a cookie, and he was trying to eat it without getting crumbs in his mustache.

Robyn felt her muscles loosen and she let out a deep

breath. What was it about this place? The obstacles on the grass. The wild poodles behind the glass door. Even the chattering of Alejandra and Jonathan and the occasional grunts of Nestor. Everything felt so easy, so effortless. It was the opposite of school. School—with the constant effort to keep it together, follow rules, and be on the lookout for trouble—was tiring. This was energizing.

"Watch out, Nestor," said Alejandra, who maybe felt the same way. She'd dropped her looking-for-a-fight edge, and now she could actually talk to Nestor without blushing. She started to giggle. "You might get *one* question of the whole page of homework wrong. You know, you're actually pretty good at fractions."

Nestor looked down and tried to hide the smile on his face.

"Hey," said Jonathan, grabbing a third cookie. "No busting Nestor's chops. Nestor has plans. He needs to be *really* good at math."

Nestor frowned. "Jonathan . . . don't."

Robyn and Alejandra leaned forward, eager to learn more.

Jonathan leaned forward too. "Nestor is going to win a Nobel Prize—maybe two. That kind of future? It doesn't just happen. You gotta be good at school, really good."

Nestor frowned and looked away.

"What?" said Jonathan. "It's true. It's a good thing."

"Ohhhh," sighed Alejandra, her eyes wide. "That's cool."

"You're gonna win a Nobel Prize?" asked Robyn. "You barely talk."

Nestor pushed out his chest. "So?"

Robyn crossed her arms. She was not buying any of this. "Did you really save a baby from a shark?"

Nestor blinked, his expression becoming unreadable.

Jonathan started laughing. "Remember? That shark was like, whoosh."

Nestor started to blush and looked down at his hands.

Jonathan said, "He also wrestled an alpaca."

"He did not," said Robyn, starting to laugh.

"Yeah. He did." Jonathan laughed even harder. "That was wild."

"People don't wrestle alpacas!" She snorted so loudly that the poodles behind Mrs. Zazueta's glass door erupted into spit-filled barks. Sundae jumped back. He ran and hid under Robyn's chair. Fudge followed him, and when she couldn't find space under the chair she jumped on Robyn's lap.

"Google 'boy wrestles alpaca, San Luis Obispo,'" said Jonathan. "You'll see."

Alejandra had already whipped out her phone.

And there it was. On YouTube. A younger-looking Nestor, with a buzz cut, wrestling a deranged-looking, half-shorn alpaca.

Robyn had to watch the short video two more times. She was laughing so hard that Fudge didn't know what to think. She jumped from Robyn's lap and started to howl. "How . . . why?"

Nestor mumbled, "It had an attitude problem."

Robyn snorted again, even louder, at which Jonathan and Alejandra burst into their own loud snorts. She had to take big, deep breaths just to calm herself.

Nestor got up from the picnic table and went to stand in front of the agility equipment.

Jonathan pulled himself together. "Okay, people. Let's start."

Nestor shot another annoyed look at his cousin. "Okay. Let's start." He went and stood on the grass and began to pace back and forth.

He said that agility had rules. It was meant for dogs like Gigante, dogs who could make everything look easy. Then he said, "So we're not going to do agility training." For once, he wasn't mumbling. His words were clear and firm. "We're going to do *ability* training."

"Ability training," said Robyn. She was still feeling giddy from all that laughing, and she remembered how she felt that day on the playground, when she'd told Nestor, Jonathan, and Alejandra about touch training. She'd known that they were about to embark on something great, and now here it was. "What's ability training?"

"It's like agility training," answered Nestor, "but it's more fun because we make it so that any dog can do it." His expression turned a little troubled and he muttered. "We're gonna make it up as we go along."

Jonathan snapped his fingers. "That's why he's gonna win a Nobel Prize. He can make stuff up. Like—kazaam—it's made."

Nestor rolled his eyes.

"Any dog can do it?" said Alejandra.

Nestor shrugged. "Well, Sundae and Fudge, because they're here. But, yeah, any dog *could* do it. That's the whole point."

"But . . . how?" asked Robyn, trying to imagine what this might look like.

Nestor told Robyn to collect Sundae and Fudge, who were once more sitting outside Mrs. Zazueta's sliding glass door, right across from the poodles.

She leashed them and brought them back to Nestor.

Nestor said they were going to take a break from the tire swing. It had spooked Fudge before, and he didn't want her to still feel spooked. Instead, they were going to try the tunnel. The tunnel was like a long nylon worm that the dogs had to run through.

They approached it like the tire swing. But this time Robyn was prepared. Using her verbal command with Sundae and her touch command for Fudge, she had the dogs sit. Then she went to the other side of the tunnel and called Sundae. He sailed straight through, and Fudge was right behind him.

The commands had worked. The dogs had learned their first obstacle.

"That was amazing!" Alejandra shouted.

Jonathan echoed her sentiments through a mouthful of both cookies and popcorn. "Sundae and Fudge are killing it!"

Robyn's eyes lit up with pride and satisfaction. She had done it. Well, Sundae and Fudge had done it, but she'd helped them get there. She looked over at Nestor, who stood looking at the dogs with his own proud expression. When he saw Robyn watching, he shook it off. "Let's go again."

They tried it again and again and again, Sundae and Fudge speeding through the tunnel every time. Then, toward the end of the lesson, Nestor said he wanted to try one more thing. This would be harder. He pointed toward the balance-beam-type structure Robyn had seen that first day in the park. It consisted of a twelve-foot-long, one-foot-wide board held up by two ramps.

"That's called a dog walk," he explained. "Sundae and Fudge will have to go up the ramp, cross the plank, and then come down the second ramp."

"Contact zone," yelled Jonathan, shoveling another handful of popcorn in his mouth.

"That's right," said Nestor. "On the way down, they've gotta touch all four paws in the contact zone."

Robyn furrowed her brow. The dog walk was one of the only obstacles that really worried her. "It looks . . . dangerous."

"It can be," said Nestor. "That's why we're going to need a little something extra." He walked over to a small cooler that Robyn hadn't noticed. He opened it and pulled out a covered container.

"No," said Jonathan, turning pale. "Anything but that."

Nestor lifted off the lid. A powerful odor began to waft around them. It was hard to identify the scent, but there was definitely a seafood component. Maybe salmon. Maybe oysters. Maybe salmon and oysters that had been left in the hot sun for a week and repeatedly peed on by cats.

Alejandra covered her face with her hands. "It smells like . . . everything bad."

"Oh my gosh," moaned Robyn, "it does." Because it did. It was the worst thing she had ever smelled in her life.

But suddenly Sundae and Fudge were jumping up on Nestor. Their nostrils flared with interest, and they made strange, pleading sounds, the likes of which Robyn had never heard before.

Stranger still, the poodles on the other side of the glass door were making the same sounds. Thin rivers of drool fell from their mouths.

"These," said Nestor, "are Grandma's secret-recipe homemade dog treats. Dogs will do anything for them."

"But they stink, Nestor. There must be some other way," begged Jonathan.

"No," said Nestor. "The stink is what makes them perfect. Between the touch commands and the smell of these treats, Fudge will be able to learn the equipment her way."

"How?" asked Alejandra.

He held up a little Velcro pouch. He attached it to the back of Sundae's harness. "I thought we could put the treat in here and train Fudge to follow the scent." That did seem pretty ingenious.

But once the pouch was attached to Sundae's harness, he kept desperately craning his neck to get at it. His eyes were so pained and his neck so crooked that they couldn't even look at him.

"How about I hold the treat in front of me," said Alejandra. "Fudge can follow my hand."

"You do not want to hold that gross stink bomb any

longer than you need to," said Jonathan. "Your hands will smell for days."

"Well . . . ," said Alejandra. "You got any barbecue tongs?"

Nestor ran and got some.

They practiced with the dogs on very short leashes, Robyn leading Sundae across the dog walk as Jonathan led Fudge. Spaced between them was Alejandra, guiding Fudge's nose forward with the stinky treat.

But the trick was getting the dogs to cross the dog walk without the leashes. Sundae, as usual, figured out what was expected of him in a snap, and he was so excited about Mrs. Zazueta's treats that he raced across the plank with confidence and ease. He didn't even wait for Fudge.

Fudge did surprisingly well too. Alejandra kept her pace slow and steady, so that the stinky treat was like a flashlight in the dark, guiding Fudge to safety. But the system wasn't perfect. Her second time doing the dog walk without a leash, Fudge veered to the left of the board and almost fell off. Jonathan rushed over and nudged her back toward the center.

"Do that," said Robyn. "Spot Fudge as she crosses the plank."

Nestor said, "Yeah. Jonathan, you be the spotter." So that became Jonathan's job.

They had the dogs practice the dog walk a few

more times before Nestor finally said they should call it a day.

Sundae and Fudge looked tired but happy. Robyn felt that way too.

"This is pretty amazing," she said.

"Well, we couldn't have done it if you hadn't learned about the touch training. That just got my brain going pop, pop, pop, pop, pop," said Nestor, more talkative than Robyn had ever seen him.

"Yeah, but using Grandma Z.'s treats. They are disgusting," said Jonathan.

"No. It was a good idea," said Robyn.

"We all had good ideas," said Alejandra. "We all helped." She had just called her dad to come pick her up, and she was putting her things back in her backpack. "I like ability training. Everyone gets to do stuff."

"And throwing out the rules too. That's pretty bold, Nestor," said Jonathan.

Nestor shrugged, but Robyn still couldn't quite believe that they were tossing out the rule book. Rules, after all, were her friends. Then again, any rules that only worked for the perfect Gigantes of the world didn't seem like very good rules.

Alejandra, Nestor, and Jonathan began chatting while they waited for Alejandra's dad to arrive. Technically, Robyn could have chatted with them. She even *wanted* to chat with them, and she knew that Nivien, who had no doubt returned and was waiting for her outside the gate, wouldn't care if she had to wait a little longer. Just the other day, when Nivien had asked Robyn about school, and Robyn had replied with a noncommittal shrug, Nivien had said, "You know, you shouldn't be afraid to talk to people. Talking is like olive oil. It makes everything go down smoother." And this would have been the perfect olive oil moment. They weren't at school. There was no Harrison looking to tear anyone down. Everyone was relaxed and happy, and no one was rushing her out the door.

It was weird. It was very, very weird. Robyn had never had any luck on teams before. She had never liked working with groups. She always felt like the outsider. Always. She was like those poodles, looking out a thick glass door at everyone else. But she didn't feel that way now. She felt like she was right alongside Nestor, Jonathan, and Alejandra. They were all on the same side of the glass. They were all looking at the same world, excited about the same world.

The problem was, she didn't understand how she'd crossed through the doorway to the other side. She didn't see how she'd managed it, or how she might manage it again, or even if it was a wholly good thing. Because . . . she had her rules to think of. And it definitely felt like the rules were still over there on the other side of the doorway. On this side of the doorway were girls who drew the wrong kind of attention to themselves, and boys who, maybe, based on what Harrison had said, drew the wrong kind of attention to themselves too.

It might be one thing if she were just moving again, like all those times in the past, she told herself. But who knew? She could end up in San Luis Obispo for the rest of her life. She wouldn't just be able to start over somewhere new next year. Any baggage she collected this early in the school year was baggage she'd be carrying for a long, long, long time. She couldn't afford that. She couldn't afford to become a grape.

Suddenly, she felt for Fudge. Because this must be what it felt like to cross a twelve-foot-long, one-foot-wide board when you could barely see a thing. But Fudge was brave. And Fudge had people to spot her. Robyn knew this: if she herself fell, there would be no one to catch her.

So she didn't linger. As Alejandra began to share another story about Argentine-school William, Robyn collected her things and her dogs, and she had Nestor let her out the gate. She heard a click as he locked the gate behind her, and when she saw Nivien waiting for her, she fell in beside her and didn't say a word.

CHAPTER 8

THE MINUTE MARSHAN AND Lulu sat down to lunch with Robyn, she knew that something was wrong, and she knew exactly what it was.

She had failed them. She had not made any progress at finding out why Alejandra wore purple.

And now they were going to tell her that they didn't want anything more to do with her. She'd seen it a million times. The friend in Boulder? The wiggly and squirmy stinker who'd sunk her reputation? He straight-out dropped her when the teacher said she talked too much. He said he couldn't be friends with someone who was so "weird." Lesson learned: people had a vision of who you were, and they didn't want you to mess with it. The wiggly and squirmy stinker had not imagined that she was the kind of person who would hog all the attention at an assembly about guide dogs. He thought she was a normal kid who liked to wiggle and squirm. When that idea was

challenged, he dumped her. Marshan and Lulu imagined that Robyn was the kind of kid who returned
favors. Now they would think she was not. They had
been so nice to her, and she hadn't even been able to
get one measly little answer out of Alejandra. They
were probably about to give her the boot.

But they just started talking about regular stuff.

Lulu mentioned how disgusting the school lunch was.

Marshan brought up an apron she'd finished making for her cat.

Then Lulu asked how the dog-training class had
gone.

"It's going good," Robyn said, forcing a smile. Because
she knew that this was just the warm-up. Pretty soon
they'd ask about why Alejandra wore purple, and she
wouldn't be able to tell them anything. She tried to
think of a way to redirect the conversation.

"Hey," said Marshan. "Maybe we can come watch
your dogs do their tricks sometime."

"Oh," said Robyn, not liking anything about how
that would mix up these two worlds she was trying so
hard to keep separate. "That would be fun."

"You know, my cat can do a trick," said Marshan.
"You can throw this little stuffed mouse at her, and
she'll bat it away."

And that was it. They were on to cats. There was no

mention of purple. There was no mention of Alejandra. It was . . . okay. No one was mad at her or ready to dump her. Everything was fine.

It dawned on her: The purple thing didn't really matter. She was actually blending in with Marshan and Lulu. She was becoming their friend. And, once again, she just felt so grateful to them. Because blending in with blender-inners? That was the dream.

The lunch assistant shooed them away. "Enough," she said. "You need to go play. You can't sit here the whole time."

And feeling like she really was one of them, Robyn again found herself walking the blacktop with Lulu and Marshan.

She spotted Alejandra, Nestor, and Jonathan over at the handball wall. Nestor was playing a boy in Robyn's class. Alejandra and Jonathan were in line. And who stood in front of them flanked by two other boys? Harrison. He wore a big smirk, and his snake eyes drilled into Jonathan, who was talking and wearing his brightest shampoo-model smile.

Alejandra's arms were crossed. She looked ready to spit.

But Jonathan kept talking and talking and talking— even after Alejandra moved up to play handball against Nestor.

Harrison's shoulders started to slump. The two other boys were looking bored, and after a moment they walked away. But Harrison stood there, still listening to Jonathan, his snake eyes looking more and more tired.

"Harrison," scoffed Marshan, noticing Robyn's gaze. "What a jerk. I can't believe what he said about you that one time."

"Yeah," said Robyn. She still didn't get why Harrison had singled her out for talking not just to Alejandra, but to Nestor and Jonathan as well, and now that she was becoming so blended in with Marshan and Lulu, she thought that maybe it would be okay to ask them.

As soon as she did, Lulu's and Marshan's eyes began to sparkle.

"Well," said Lulu, the words falling eagerly from her mouth. "We've thought about it."

"A lot!" said Marshan. "A *whole* lot. We think he was like, 'What? Does Robyn think she's like some great Moringa or something?'"

"A Moringa is a very helpful tree," explained Lulu. "People can eat parts of it. It's good in droughts, and its seeds can purify water."

"Right," said Marshan. "So Harrison was like, 'Oh, you think you're *so* helpful, being nice to all the people with all the sad stories. You must think you're *so* perfect.'" She spoke in a high-pitched, sarcastic voice, making it clear that she did not believe Harrison thought anything of the kind.

"But what's so sad about Nestor and Jonathan?"

Marshan and Lulu looked at her in surprise.

"Don't you know?" said Marshan. "Nestor had cancer. And Jonathan's his cousin, so, you know, it was hard on him too."

Robyn's breath caught in her throat. "Wait . . . what?" She had not met anyone with cancer. But she'd heard of the disease. Her mom had friends who researched it, and sometimes, when they visited, she'd hear them say how hard it was to fight. For some people, it was a death sentence. For others, it was an unpleasant chapter in their lives.

Lulu's and Marshan's heads were bobbing up and down.

"It was a while ago," said Marshan. "But still, that kind of a thing sticks to a person."

Robyn did a double take. "You mean . . . he doesn't have cancer now. Does he?"

"I don't think so," continued Marshan. "But everyone knows he's the kid who had cancer."

"It's sad," said Lulu.

Robyn looked over at Nestor. She would never be able to tell by looking at him that he had had cancer. Heck, even during all their time doing agility together she never would have guessed it. But still, she wondered if Marshan was right. Was that who Nestor was? Was that who he would always be?

"Didn't you ever see the video of him wrestling a goat?" Marshan asked.

"Alpaca," Robyn answered. "What's that got to do with anything?"

Lulu reached out her hand and squeezed Robyn's wrist. "It was some cancer kid thing. Like, if you can wrestle a goat, you can beat cancer."

Marshan looked grief-stricken. "They don't let regular kids wrestle goats. That would be cruelty to animals."

The bell rang, and Robyn walked numbly back to class. Part of her wondered if Lulu and Marshan were wrong about Nestor being a cancer survivor. But most of her believed them, and she suddenly felt worried for, and protective of, Nestor. She found herself shaking her head, as if she were shaking off everything she'd just learned. But you can't shake off something like that. And even though she knew she didn't consider Nestor a friend—knew that she shouldn't consider him a friend—it saddened her to realize that she'd never even wondered if there was more to him than met the eye.

The class was working on math, and Robyn looked up to see Alejandra all alone, her desk mates crowded around Mrs. Wang. Every bone in Robyn's body knew that this was school: she needed to ignore Alejandra. But every bone in her body also knew that she would not be able to rest until she understood what had happened to Nestor.

And she knew too that this was a place where her two worlds *could* collide, at least a little. Because Lulu and Marshan—so nice—would want to know as much about this cancer business as her. She mumbled to Lulu and Marshan, "I'll be right back. I'm going to figure out this Nestor/cancer thing."

Their eyes grew wide. "Yeah, do that," said Marshan.

Robyn nodded and slunk quietly to Alejandra's desk.

"Hey!" said Alejandra, happy for the visit. "You never come see me in class."

Suddenly, Harrison slid back into his seat right next to Alejandra. He leaned forward and looked at Robyn. He said, "I got my eye on you, New Kid."

Robyn pulled her head back, instantly performing the mental calculations she was so good at. Laugh it off? Don't be a pushover? Burn everything down? No! *Definitely* don't burn everything down.

"Ah, your mother cooks rice one grain at a time, you animal," said Alejandra, an acid tone in her voice.

"Yeah, well, your mother is as purple as you, you giant purple Popsicle."

Alejandra poked her finger hard into his arm. "Don't you make fun of my mother."

He let out a soft "Owwww," and turned back to his work.

Robyn whispered in Alejandra's ear, "Did you know Nestor had cancer?"

Alejandra nodded gravely. "Yeah. In second grade. Jonathan told me. That's one reason he's Nestor's business manager. He's kind of made it his job to look out for Nestor." She lowered her voice. "But don't tell Nestor. He hates when Jonathan does that."

Robyn couldn't help herself. She leaned in closer. "Why does wrestling an alpaca prove you can beat cancer?"

That one had Alejandra stumped. She said they could ask Nestor at recess.

Robyn leaned forward. She could see that Harrison was watching them from the corner of his eyes. It was then that Robyn realized what made his eyes so snakelike. It was his eyelashes. They were stubby and completely white. From a distance, they seemed nonexistent.

Alejandra had noticed him watching them too. She spat, "Mind your own business, Harrison."

"Go hang from a vine, Grape," he answered.

Robyn glanced over at Lulu and Marshan. They were watching her, their heads tottering up and down like bobblehead dolls.

"Okay," she said, and then rushed back to her desk.

"What did you learn?" asked Marshan, full of worry.

"Nothing new," said Robyn. "Just that Jonathan feels like he has to look after Nestor."

"That's so sad," said Lulu, surprised.

"Poor Jonathan," said Marshan.

"I'm going to find out a little more at recess," offered Robyn. "I'm going to ask about the alpaca . . . goat."

Marshan and Lulu gasped and grabbed each other's hands.

"Do that," said Marshan.

Lulu reached her free hand across the desks and grabbed Robyn's. "What did Harrison say to you?"

She shrugged. "Nothing I couldn't handle."

"I see Harrison bugging Alejandra all the time now," said Lulu, frowning.

"He's the worst," added Marshan.

Afternoon recess came, and Lulu and Marshan encouraged Robyn on. "Hurry," urged Marshan. "You don't have much time."

Robyn rushed to Alejandra and they ran together to Nestor and Jonathan, who were heading to the handball line.

When they reached them, Alejandra bent over

and panted. She said, "Why does wrestling an alpaca prove you can beat cancer?"

She asked it so fearlessly and directly that Robyn worried that Nestor might go all Bruce on her, but he and Jonathan burst out laughing.

Finally, Jonathan said, "Who told you that?"

Robyn admitted that it had been Lulu and Marshan.

Jonathan muttered, "Figures." Then he said, "Nestor wasn't wrestling it. He was shaving the wool off it. But he was really bad at it."

Alejandra giggled. "I bet Nestor wasn't so bad."

Nestor slid his hand into his pockets. "No. I was bad. And those alpaca like to mooove."

Robyn smiled. "You always sound like a cow when you say that."

His face turned pink, and he glanced down at his shoes. Then he shrugged. "The alpaca thing was part of a hospital program for kids with cancer. It was for us to get to know each other and stuff. It was no big deal."

Robyn's smile fell away. It seemed like a big deal.

"What about the baby and the shark?" asked Alejandra. "Did you really save a baby?"

Jonathan and Nestor started laughing again.

Jonathan explained that Nestor and his dad had gone kayaking. "They saw the fin of a great white, which was kind of unusual but not super unusual. His dad was all, 'We better head back.' So they headed back, and they saw this guy and his kid on a paddle-board."

He pointed his finger like he was acting Nestor's part. "And Nestor said"—here Jonathan made his voice as gruff and mumbly as Nestor's—"'Shark.'" He started to laugh again. "He was just trying to warn them. You know?"

Jonathan started to laugh harder. And soon he had to stop talking every few words just to let more laughter out.

And the more Jonathan laughed, the more Alejandra laughed, and—at the sight of both of them yukking it up, Robyn couldn't help herself. She started to laugh too.

All the while, Nestor stood there, his hands in his pockets, a little half smile pulling up one side of his mouth as his face grew pinker, and pinker, and even pinker.

Jonathan said, "The kid . . . It was so funny. . . . He's screaming and crying at the top of his lungs. . . . I could see him from the shore. . . . And the guy . . . the dad . . . he's trying to keep them both from falling off the paddleboard."

He took a few breaths. "So the paddleboard started tipping, and the dad tries to stop it, and—boom—there they go into the water. And now the kid is really, really freaking out, and his little orange life vest is bobbing up and down, and the guy is out there trying to push the kid back onto the paddleboard, but the kid is splashing all over the place. And the shark is totally long gone by now.

"So Nestor's dad paddles over there, and they pull the kid onto the kayak, and the guy gets back on the paddleboard. And the whole time they're all coming back, the kid was saying . . . Nestor, what was he saying?"

The other corner of Nestor's mouth sprang up. "He said, 'I felt the shark. It almost got me. It almost got me.'"

And that was it—Jonathan was busting up again. A tear rolled down his face, and he whisked it away. "'I felt the shark! It almost got me! It almost got me!'"

Alejandra was laughing so hard that she fell onto the ground and rolled on her back.

A yard duty assistant pointed at them. "No lying down on the blacktop."

Jonathan put out his hand and pulled Alejandra up, as all four of them fell into hysterics.

Alejandra waved her hands up and down and squeezed her thighs together. "I'm gonna pee my pants! I'm gonna pee my pants."

Robyn, Nestor, and Jonathan laughed even harder, and Robyn felt a release in her chest as all that sound and vibration left her body.

She looked up. Her breath caught in her throat. A girl Robyn often saw eating with Nestor was watching them. She had chocolate-colored skin, and she wore glasses and used arm braces. Two other girls playing basketball were also watching them. And everyone in the handball line was watching them. And Marshan and Lulu. And of all the people who were watching them, Marshan and Lulu were watching them the most closely. Their lips were tight, and panic shone from their eyes. When they realized Robyn was looking at them, their eyes popped wide, and they looked pointedly from her to something behind her and then back at her again.

She turned her head. There stood Harrison. His feet were planted widely on the ground and his arms were crossed. He was staring right at her.

A ball of nervousness started jumping around in her belly. That made it twice in one day that she'd caught Harrison looking at her.

"Blend in!" shouted the ball in her tummy. "You're attracting too much attention—too much *bad* attention. Hit the road, lady."

She was still smiling, but now an anxious tremor shook her mouth. She said, "That's so funny . . . um . . ." She turned to Nestor. "But you're completely better now, right? You don't have cancer anymore?"

He shook his head.

Jonathan put his arm around his cousin. "That cancer is gone, and it's never coming back. Huh, Nestor?"

Nestor shrugged, his expression turning blank.

Robyn took a step. "Okay. Good. Um . . . I'll see you later." And with that, she ran back to Lulu and Marshan.

"Tell us everything," insisted Lulu.

She spilled it all out, but they didn't think the story about the shark was funny.

"I don't get it," said Marshan. "It wasn't even a baby."

And they did think that Harrison staring at her was a bad sign, a very bad sign.

Lulu kept biting her knuckles. "Oh my gosh, what if he says something to you? What would he even say? I would be so stressed right now. Are you stressed? Are you stressing out? Poor you. I'd be so worried."

"Me too," said Marshan, looking at her friend and then at Robyn. "I would be so, so worried."

And because Lulu and Marshan were worried, Robyn was worried. Lesson learned. It was time to be worried. It was time to not just have a boundary between the worlds of school and dog training. It was time to make that boundary a concrete wall.

CHAPTER 9

THE IMPENETRABLE WALL WAS built. Everything school on one side. Everything dog-training on the other. Robyn tried harder than ever to avoid Alejandra, Nestor, and Jonathan at school. Rules were followed. Rules were good.

But ability training was better.

By October, Robyn and the dogs had learned a lot. They could do the tunnel, the dog walk, and the pause table (a table dogs had to wait on until directed otherwise). They could even do the tire swing. (The key for Fudge? Moving slowly enough that she could see the bottom of the tire and then step over it.) And once the dogs could do the tire swing, it was no problem to teach them the other agility jump: the hurdle.

"Sundae and Fudge are more confident since they started ability training. Don't you think? They're happier too," said Alejandra one day at Nestor's house. It was fully autumn now. There was a chill in the air, and the ground was covered with orange-and-yellow leaves that they'd had to rake up before they could begin so that the dogs wouldn't slip on them or get distracted by their scents.

They had just finished their math homework. In general, math was going better for all of them, unless there were word problems. Both Robyn and Jonathan really needed Alejandra's help with the word problems.

A tray of Rice Krispies treats lay before them. Robyn had made them herself. She was really getting into the snack-making now, trying every week to bring something new and yummy. She felt particularly proud of the Rice Krispies treats, knowing, as she did, that they were one of the greatest desserts of all time, and their mere presence in a room brought oohs and aahs and excited glances.

"Sundae and Fudge are happier," said Robyn, "because they're more confident." She told them how Fudge, once a big pushover with Sundae, never let him boss her around anymore. If he tried to nudge her out of the way of extra food or belly rubs, she nudged him right back. If he tried to crowd her off a lap or chair, she would dig into her position and stay. And if he tried to take her matted and slobbery stuffed ladybug? Good luck! She would grasp it in her mouth, growl, and show him the tops of her teeth.

Nestor said, "Fudge is more confident. Sundae still seems pretty anxious."

Robyn shook her head. "No. Sundae is more confident too. He doesn't even need Fudge near him when he does the obstacles anymore. He does them all by himself."

"That's because he's greedy," Nestor replied. "He wants my grandma's snacks."

At the sound of his name, Sundae had run to Robyn. Now he was staring at the bag of stinky treats in her hand.

"Are you just greedy?" said Alejandra, plopping next to Robyn and petting Sundae. "Are you a greedy boy?"

Robyn thought about Sundae. Not so long ago, he'd cowered at the sight and sound of the poodles on the other side of the window. Now he watched them like they didn't matter one speck. "No," she said. "He's more confident too."

Just then there was a knock at the gate.

Inside Mrs. Zazueta's house, the poodles erupted. They started barking and scratching at the glass.

Nestor ran over to the gate and opened it.

A round boy with pale skin, deep-set eyes, and a cowlick that made the back of his hair stick straight up walked in. He had with him a pit bull with three legs.

Alejandra ran over to him. "William!"

William? thought Robyn. William from Argentine school? What was he doing there?

William had a pastry box with him. He walked it over to the outdoor dining table, smiling while Jonathan explained that William and his dog were joining the class.

"It was my idea," hollered Alejandra. "As soon as Nestor said that we were going to do a kind of training that any dog could do, I thought to myself, *Well, what about Tiger? Tiger would probably like this as much as Sundae and Fudge.* So then I asked Nestor, because of course I couldn't invite William and Tiger without permission. Nestor thought it was a great idea, and William thought it was a great idea too. But then William fell in a ditch while trying to escape some crows who hate him, and he sprained his ankle and couldn't come. But now he's better, aren't you, William?"

William looked around and nodded.

"And so here we all are!" exclaimed Alejandra.

But Robyn had tuned Alejandra out. She was staring at that pastry box. It smelled of something warm and meaty, but what exactly was in there? She brought the snack. She always brought the snack. That was her important contribution.

Suddenly, there was a rumbling sound. Robyn looked up. Bruce's open mouth was headed straight toward them. At least it seemed that way. His legs lurched left while his skull lurched right. Then his head lurched right while his legs lurched left. The two slightly less-enormous poodles ran behind him. They weren't lurching anywhere, and they made things very clear: the poodles were coming for William.

"Bruce," said Jonathan, fury blazing in his eyes.

From the corner of her own eyes, Robyn saw Sundae, Fudge, and the pit bull slip under the table as Bruce leaped in the air and landed on William, knocking him to the ground. The dog's bottom slid right onto William's face, and he stayed there, trapping William's writhing body underneath him.

The second poodle snatched the pastry box in its jaws as the third ran back and forth in front of Nestor, Robyn, and the others.

Then the second poodle, followed by the third, ran back into Mrs. Zazueta's house as Bruce leaped off William and, lurching once more, ran inside himself.

Nestor was right behind him, yelling, "Abuelo!"

Jonathan stepped forward. He was shaking his fist in the air. "Bruce. He's their leader. Last year, he stole my birthday cake."

William stood up, stunned. "What just happened?"

"The poodles stole your box, man. They planned it all out too. I hate those dogs."

"I'm sure they didn't plan it," said Alejandra.

Sundae, Fudge, and the pit bull emerged from under the table and began sniffing the ground where William had fallen.

"Dogs are smart," added Alejandra. "But they're not *that* smart."

"Believe me," said Jonathan, crossing his arms. "They knew what they were doing."

He nodded at William. "I bet there was something good in that box too."

"Beef empanadas."

Jonathan moaned. "I love empanadas."

"William's parents own an Argentine restaurant," said Alejandra. "It's really good."

"That's what did it," said Jonathan. "When they smell something really good, they find a way to steal it."

"They never did that with my snacks," said Robyn.

But no one seemed to be listening to her. They were all staring at the sliding glass door. On the other side of the glass, pieces of the pink pastry box lay strewn about, all hints of its contents gone except for one greasy piece of tissue paper dangling from Bruce's mouth. The dogs were lined up as usual, victory spread across their faces.

"There is a storm a-comin' for you, Bruce," hissed Jonathan. "One day. You'll see."

Nestor ran outside. He was shaking his head, frowning. "I don't know where my grandpa is. Sometimes it takes him a little longer to help Grandma set up her classes. He might still be at the park. Maybe he left the kitchen door open a little."

"No," said Jonathan. "It was Bruce. Bruce tricked him somehow."

William was shaking his head. "No big deal. I'll bring more empanadas next time. But . . . um . . . what was with the . . ." He lurched his arms one way, then another.

"Inner-ear problem," said Nestor.

Jonathan shook his head. "It's all part of Bruce's act. That dog's an evil genius."

Everything had happened so fast. Too fast. Part of Robyn was still back in that moment when William walked in the gate. She tried to make sense of what she knew. So William was taking the class too now. Okay. Whatever. But had no one thought to mention it to her? And what was with the empanadas? She liked empanadas, but was William always going to bring them? Because the snack was her thing. And everyone had seemed fine with the snack being her thing until now.

"So how is this going to work?" she asked Nestor.

He said that Robyn and Sundae were ready to practice a lot of the course by themselves. The same was true for Alejandra and Jonathan when it came to Fudge. While the three of them worked with Sundae and Fudge, Nestor would teach William and Tiger. He was going to start them on the tunnel. Then, while William and Tiger were practicing that, he'd introduce the rest of them to the weave poles.

The weave poles were the slalom-skiing-type poles she'd seen the day she stumbled upon Mrs. Zazueta's class. The poles were arranged in a straight line, and the goal was to get the dogs to weave in and out of them one after the other. They were one of the hardest tasks on the course.

Robyn didn't see how Nestor would be able to help them learn the weave poles if he was also helping William and Tiger learn the tunnel. But everyone else seemed fine with this arrangement, so she didn't know what to say, and not knowing what to say, she just tried to focus on learning the obstacle.

But the weave poles were hard. Following Nestor's directions, Robyn attempted to lure Sundae in and out of the poles with a stinky treat. She was basically doing what Jonathan and Robyn always did with Fudge, and, in fact, Fudge, as usual, was doing great. But Sundae didn't like it. If the treat was going to be right in front of him, he couldn't figure out why he shouldn't be able to just grab it out of Robyn's hand, so he kept lunging for it. Likewise, he didn't understand why anyone wanted him to weave in and out of the poles. One side of his mouth would pull up in confusion every time Robyn tried to coax him between them, as if to say, "Who cares about these poles? Why can't I just run in a straight line?"

She needed help. She glanced left. There were Alejandra and Jonathan, looking tight as could be at the other end of the weave poles. She glanced right: There were Nestor and William. They had only just met. Yet anyone would have thought they'd been friends forever. The way they talked. The way they carried themselves. They seemed so natural with each other.

They made it look so uncomplicated. The connecting. The friending. All four of them did.

She wondered if it was something they were born with. Or if maybe things were different if you didn't move all the time, if your feet were planted firmly on the ground where everyone else's feet were also firmly planted and had always been firmly planted. Whatever it was, she knew she didn't have that particular brand of magic, that knack for easiness around people she didn't know.

And she felt, suddenly, very alone. Because if a radioactive girl had that magic, and if a boy who would always be the kid who had cancer had that magic, and if a sixth grader who fell into pies and ditches, and was sat on by wild poodles, had that magic, then what did that say about her?

Her body drooped, just a little, as she let out a small

breath. Then she called Sundae, and they tried the weave poles again.

When class ended, she gathered her things and leashed up the dogs even quicker than usual. As the gate closed behind her, she could hear Alejandra and William talking away to Jonathan and Nestor, like they didn't even care that she'd left, like her presence didn't matter one bit. And it shouldn't have bothered her. They weren't her real friends. They weren't even people she talked to at school. They were just people she had an exchange of services with. But for some unknown reason, it really, really bothered her.

CHAPTER 10

THAT NIGHT, BEFORE ROBYN went to bed, she looked at the list of new-kid rules still pinned to her bulletin board. The scientific, logical part of her knew that these were good, commonsense rules. They were rules to live by, rules that had been tested and tried in a variety of scenarios, places, and situations. So why weren't they working the way they were supposed to? Why was she feeling dissatisfied and restless?

At school the next day, Lulu and Marshan seemed to sense that something was wrong, but when they asked her about it, she didn't even know how to explain. So she shrugged and said, "I'm okay."

They weren't buying it. They pressed her again at lunch.

"Are you sure you're not sad?" asked Lulu, her brows perched high on her head.

"You seem a little quiet," added Marshan.

But it wasn't sadness she was feeling. It was

something sharper and grumpier than sadness. And suddenly all she wanted was to move her body.

"Hey," she said. "You guys want to play handball? I love handball."

Lulu cringed. "Handball gets you so sweaty."

"Yeah," said Marshan. "And the ball makes your hand all dirty."

Robyn said, "Okay. Well, I kind of feel like doing that today. So . . . I'm going to do that." She paused for a second before adding, "Is that okay?"

Lulu's shoulders rolled up and down. "Do what you want."

"Yeah," said Marshan. "Have fun."

Robyn ran to the handball wall. She wondered if she would find her dog-training group there. She often saw them playing handball. She kind of hoped, but also didn't hope, that she would.

Sure enough, there they were, in line. Jonathan and Nestor stood on either side of Alejandra. They had big grins on their faces as Alejandra, who must have been telling some whopper of a story, waved her hands in the air and jumped up and down. And the three of them just looked so close, and she knew that if she joined them in line, she would make it weird for all of them. Because you couldn't fake some things, like connectedness. She wasn't one of them. She hadn't wanted to be, and she had gotten what she wanted.

And Robyn . . . just couldn't do it. Without stopping, she did a U-turn and ran right back to Marshan and Lulu. "I changed my mind. Wanna walk around?"

The lunch assistant hollered, "Yes. Walk around. Eating time is over. I have to clean this table. Get up. Go."

And so they walked around the blacktop, and Robyn's feet felt heavy as Marshan started to show off the latest scratches from her cat, who very much seemed to hate the pumpkin costume she had sewn for it.

"But I just don't understand why," said Marshan. "It's so cute."

Over the next few days, Robyn found her eyes searching for Nestor, Jonathan, and Alejandra at least once during every recess. She wanted to know: Were they always together? Were they always so . . . happy?

Mostly they were. At least it seemed like that. And every time she realized it, she felt a lump in her stomach and a strange sense of disappointment, until one day it hit her like a tumbling pile of bricks: She didn't want a wall between them. She didn't want a world of school and a world of dog training. She wanted one world. She wanted their world. And she didn't care about Harrison. She didn't care about anyone. She just wanted to get back to the other side of the wall so she could be with them. Because she liked them. She liked them a lot, and maybe that was all that mattered. Maybe that was enough reason to let everything else go.

The only problem was, she didn't know how to climb the wall she herself had built.

But then Alejandra signaled a way.

They were walking to Nestor's with the dogs, Nivien keeping her usual six feet behind them.

Alejandra said, "Did you know that the whole reason Nestor wants to win a Nobel Prize is because he had cancer? When his cancer was all the way gone, he was like, 'I guess I better do something awesome with my life because I might have died.'"

"That sounds like a lot of words for Nestor," said Robyn. The words came out snarkier than she'd meant them, but Alejandra didn't seem to notice one way or another.

"He talks a lot, actually. You know what else? The Nobel Prize thing is another reason Jonathan decided to become Nestor's business manager. He says if Nestor's getting the big Nobel Prize bucks, he wants his cut."

"Now, that does sound like Jonathan," Robyn answered, snarkier yet, and this time kicking herself for it, knowing that being snarky would only widen the gap between them, not close it. But she just couldn't seem to help herself.

Alejandra kept right on talking. "But guess what else? The cancer thing is also why Jonathan made his first big business manager decision of saying we should exchange math tutoring for agility lessons, because Nestor still feels bad that his having cancer cost his family a bunch of money. I didn't know it, but it's really expensive to have cancer. Did you know that? And did you know that Nestor's mom and Jonathan's mom are identical twins? And that their family has been living in California since the early eighteen hundreds? They used to have a great big ranch."

The shadows on her face seemed to grow darker, and a fierceness lit up her eyes. "People spoke Spanish in California before they even spoke English, you know."

Robyn didn't respond. She didn't know what to say, and she didn't trust herself.

And that was when Alejandra offered her the lifeline. She said, "Hey, we thought you were going to play handball with us earlier in the week. We saw you running toward us. Why didn't you?"

Too embarrassed to tell the truth, Robyn muttered, "Oh, I just changed my mind."

"Well, you should play sometime. You're good at handball, and honestly, I kind of would like a bit more of a challenge sometimes. The other people who play are all right, but not as good as us."

"Okay," said Robyn, perking up. "I've missed playing handball."

"Oh, and you should come trick-or-treating with us. We were going to invite you when we saw you, but then you ran the other way." She shook her head. "We were like, 'What's that all about?'"

"It was nothing," said Robyn, her heart beating faster. Because there it was. An invitation to their side of the wall. But Halloween was tricky. It was Mom's birthday, and they had a tradition of spending the evening together. The habit was born as much from Robyn usually having no one to trick-or-treat with as from any birthday wishes of Mom's, and Robyn knew she could bail on Mom if she really wanted to. But she liked spending Halloween with Mom. They watched spooky movies, handed out candy, and sat on the couch while eating pizza and ice cream birthday cake. She couldn't imagine not doing those things. And then she remembered Sundae. Doorbells and trick-or-treaters freaked him out. Either she or Mom normally held him while the other passed out the candy. So that made trick-or-treating hard too.

She explained these things to Alejandra, who shrugged and said, "I get it. If it were my mom I would stay home for sure."

But Robyn didn't want to lose that invitation either.

This was her chance to make things right, to get where she wanted to be. She had an idea. "You guys could stop by my house! I can make it like a mini-party." The perfection of the plan began to unfurl before her. She could be with Mom. She could help out with Sundae. She could bond with Alejandra, Nestor, and Jonathan. And bonus: there would be no prying eyes of Harrison or anyone else to make her doubt herself or her wishes.

"Okay, that sounds fun!" said Alejandra, skipping once and then once more.

"Okay," said Robyn, suddenly even more excited about Halloween.

When they reached Nestor's, William was already there, and his box of empanadas was wide open.

Jonathan was standing in front of Mrs. Zazueta's sliding glass door. He was eating his empanada right in front of Bruce, whose mouth kept twitching, revealing the bright white of his teeth.

"I love these," said Alejandra, biting into an empanada of her own.

Robyn did not take an empanada. Instead, she opened her backpack and pulled out a bag of homemade Chex Mix. It was the kind she and Mom made every Christmas. They added extra peanuts and—for an inspired bit of tasty delight—Bugles. It was famously good. Whenever Mom brought it to work, the other people in the biology department went wild. Robyn set it on the table and then—for a double wow factor—she pulled out some extra-fudgy brownies that she'd made from a mix and topped with chocolate chips.

She looked up at everyone, her eyes alight with expectation.

But they were still focused on the empanadas.

"I brought snacks too," she said, smiling and gesturing at the treats she'd worked so hard to make.

Alejandra glanced at the Chex Mix and brownies. "Those look good, but I'm full right now."

"Me too," said Nestor, wiping his hands on a paper towel.

Jonathan pointed at the brownies. "I'll have one of those."

Her smile faltered. She'd hoped for a better reaction, and maybe some stampeding poodles, but she barreled ahead and, as they pulled out their math work, she asked the rest of the ability class if they wanted to drop by her house when they went trick-or-treating. "I'm gonna make it really special," she said. "It'll be more than trick-or-treating. It'll be fun."

Nestor and William both said, "Sure."

Like with her snack, it wasn't the reaction she'd been looking for, but it was fine. She barely knew

William, and when was Nestor ever enthusiastic about anything?

Jonathan seemed suspicious. He said, "You're not going to be giving out any of this Laffy Taffy business, right? Because I don't like no Laffy Taffy. I'm a chocolate man through and through."

Robyn promised there would be chocolate.

He pushed out his lower lip. "Okay. We'll be there."

And she was true to her word. When Halloween arrived, she had a bowl filled with Kit Kats, M&M's, and Reese's Peanut Butter Cups. But that wasn't all. Robyn had gone all out. She had made more Rice Krispies treats. This time, she topped them with black and orange sprinkles and used a greased cookie cutter to shape them into pumpkins. And, of course, there was ice cream cake: chocolate ice cream atop a chocolate-cookie crust, with whipped cream and fudge on the top.

But the food was the least of it. Best of all was the vibe. She had gotten a black cloak, and she made Mom make up her face like a skeleton. When they rang the bell, she was going to jump out holding Sundae. He was going to be donning a devil-horns headband. And when they saw her, she was going to cackle and say, "We've been waiting for you!" It would be just like Mrs. Zazueta's talking skeleton. They would all laugh so much.

Then, as planned, she would usher them to her bedroom-turned-haunted-house. She'd worked all day to make it super spooky, with a dim orange light shining from her elephant lamp, pillows arranged under her covers to look like a body, construction-paper bats hanging from her ceiling, and a plastic ghost ready to pop out from her closet as soon as she pulled a string attached to the doorknob. Also, in an extra dose of cuteness, there would be Fudge, wearing a little witch's hat and sitting on the floor next to a Magic 8 Ball. Robyn was going to have everyone ask the Magic 8 Ball a spooky question, and then she was going to give them all a little treat bag to take home.

It was perfect.

That night, Robyn's heart jumped with excitement every time the doorbell rang. She practically ran to the door, hoping it was them. But with each witch or superhero or vampire or character she didn't recognize, Robyn's hope waned. By the last trick-or-treater, her heart had sunk. She didn't even bother going to the door. She just lay on the couch, holding Sundae and trying to keep him calm.

"Well, we're officially out of candy," Mom said, returning from the front door with an empty bowl in her hand. "I'm so sorry your friends didn't show up, sweetie."

"It doesn't matter," Robyn replied, rule number

nine suddenly appearing in her head: If they hurt you, don't let it show. "They can do what they want. We're just business partners."

Sundae squirmed as Mom came and sat down next to her, and Fudge—at Robyn's feet—toddled straight over Robyn so that she could have a lap of her own.

Mom rested one hand on Fudge and another on Robyn's head. Combing her fingers through Robyn's hair, she said, "Well . . . you seemed pretty excited."

Her voice tight, Robyn said, "I was just trying to be nice to them. It didn't matter to me."

Mom didn't look convinced, but she didn't press it and just restarted the movie they'd been watching. It wasn't really that spooky, just *Pirates of the Caribbean*, which was one of Mom's favorites. But the fun was gone, and after a while Robyn excused herself, saying she was tired.

She washed the makeup off her face and put on her pajamas. Then she got rid of everything: the paper bats, the ghost in the closet. She kicked the Magic 8 Ball under her bed. Magic 8 Balls were stupid anyway. And she replaced the orange-hued lightbulb with a regular one.

Sundae and Fudge lay on her bed, their eyes closed.

When she was done, she lay next to them. "It's okay," she told them. "We don't need them."

She turned off her light and tossed one way and then another, trying to take a little more space on the bed from Fudge, the big bed hog. Then she sighed. "But I did think maybe they wanted to be friends with us. I guess I was wrong." She sniffled, and Sundae lifted his head and licked her cheek. Then Fudge pushed Robyn's head against the wall, but in a loving way. "Thank you," she said. "You can always count on me too."

Business. It was all business the next day at ability class. For snack, she brought pretzels. Who cared? They would probably only want to eat William's empanadas anyway. When it was math time, she did her math work. She wasn't even going to mention Halloween. Why bother? They had their little group. She wasn't in it. She would never be in it. That was that.

She tried not to listen when they talked about some street they had gone to where everyone was handing out full-size candy bars. Apparently, they had learned about it from Harrison.

That part she couldn't ignore. "Harrison? Why would you even talk to him? He's mean to Alejandra."

"He's not so bad," said Alejandra.

Robyn's mouth fell open. "All he does is make fun of you."

Alejandra rolled her eyes. "And then I make fun of him. It's our thing."

"What you need to know about Harrison," said Jonathan, "is that he's complicated. He's like fractions. He has many parts."

"That's right," said Alejandra. "It's like, he *can* be a jerk, but only because he's sort of a doofus and has a big mouth. You've just kind of got to put him back in his place when he gets out of line." She pointed her finger and made a face like she was giving him a stink eye. Afterward, she shrugged. "Then he's pretty nice. He has a little dachshund that falls asleep when it gets too excited. He loves it so much."

Robyn couldn't believe what she was hearing. She shook her head. "Marshan and Lulu say he's a jerk. They say he's always been a jerk. One time, he saw me with you guys, and he said, 'Who does that new girl think she is?' And he meant it in a real judgey way because he's a judger."

Jonathan sighed. "I wouldn't listen too much to Marshan and Lulu if I were you. They're a couple of gossip sniffers."

Robyn stood up, suddenly feeling very angry. "Well, at least they're nice. They're my friends. And I can't believe you would listen to Harrison but not even come by my house like you said you would!"

Oops. She had let it show. She had let them see

how much they'd hurt her. She sat back down and readjusted her ponytail. More calmly, she said, "Not that it matters. I'm just saying."

"Umm," said William, a guilty look on his face. "I guess we forgot."

"It's not so much that we forgot," said Jonathan. "But . . . there were full-size candy bars on the street we were telling you about. We couldn't get those and come to your house too. I'm telling you, they were *full-size*. Anyone would have made that choice. It's nothing personal."

Robyn crossed her legs primly at the ankle and rested her hands on her lap. "Well, you could have texted."

Jonathan shook his head. "Nestor and I don't have phones."

"Me neither," said William.

Alejandra was slumped down near the end of the table. "Sorry. I didn't think of it."

Robyn could feel tears pricking at the back of her eyes and willed them to stay put. "Like I said, it's fine."

"We are sorry," Alejandra continued. "To be honest, we didn't really think you'd care."

William and Jonathan nodded, but Nestor was giving Robyn a strange look, like he wanted to see what she'd do next. Like he thought maybe she *did* care and was trying to hide it.

Robyn looked down. She ran her sleeve across her nose and shrugged. "No. I didn't care."

After a moment of awkward quiet, Nestor stood up too. He clapped his hands. "It's time for work."

"Right," said Robyn, sounding businesslike and independent and not at all like a person who still had a plate of pumpkin-shaped Rice Krispies treats at home. "That's why we're here."

Nestor told William to practice the tunnel with Tiger. He wanted to get Sundae and Fudge started on something new. The roof-shaped A-frame.

While Jonathan and Alejandra were getting Fudge harnessed up, Nestor came over to Robyn and whispered, "Are you sure you're okay?"

A lump formed in the back of Robyn's throat. Of course she wasn't okay. She had worked really hard on cooking for them and decorating her room. She'd really, really looked forward to them coming to her house, and they'd bailed on her. She was less important to them than a full-size candy bar. She might as well have been Laffy Taffy.

"Yes," Robyn said, keeping her eyes on Sundae's harness as she pretended to adjust it. "I told you. It's fine. You guys do you. It's not like we're friends."

There. She had said what they were all thinking. What they had said loud and clear when they didn't show up at her house. There was no reason to pretend this was anything other than a business arrangement anymore.

Nestor still stood next to her, silent. Finally, a little gruffer than usual, he said, "Right. Fine." And he walked away.

"If a dog is going to get hurt," said Nestor, now loud enough for Jonathan and Alejandra to hear, "it's probably going to be on the A-frame." For that reason, he planned on spotting Fudge along with Jonathan. Like with the dog walk, they practiced first with the dogs on their leashes. They walked them up and down the obstacle, rewarding them with Mrs. Zazueta's dog treats when they reached the bottom.

Soon, Sundae was ready to try it off-leash. He practiced it a few times, but he was starting to get bossy about the treats, bumping Fudge out of his way before she could do the obstacle herself.

"Run the course with Sundae," Nestor told Robyn, explaining that he wanted to keep working with Fudge, Jonathan, and Alejandra. "Do the tire swing, hurdle, pause table, dog walk, weave poles, and tunnel."

Fine, thought Robyn. Combining obstacles into a mini agility course was Robyn's favorite part of class. She loved directing Sundae from one piece of equipment to the next. But this time she didn't love it. It felt like a chore. More than that, it felt like Halloween—like she'd been purposely excluded and ignored.

Her voice flat, she directed Sundae from obstacle to obstacle. They were struggling, again, with the weave poles when the backyard suddenly filled with loud, prancing poodles. Her eyes grew big as Sundae turned around and made a running leap into her arms. She caught him and looked up to see a new figure.

It was Mrs. Zazueta. Her silver hair was shining as she stood in front of the open glass door. Gigante sat by her side, Buddha-like as ever. But Mrs. Zazueta was definitely not Buddha-like. Mrs. Zazueta's face was turning redder and redder, and if she were a volcano she would have started to erupt.

"Nestor Zazueta," said the woman, her voice a low and steely growl. "Explain."

CHAPTER 11

THE MOVEMENT IN THE yard came to a halt. The only sound was Bruce, who was looking at the pastry box and taking big, loud sniffs. But even Bruce knew not to test his luck with Mrs. Zazueta around. He stood where he was.

Nestor stepped forward. He mumbled, "Ummm..."

"How you doing, Grandma Z.?" said Jonathan brightly. "We invited a few friends and their dogs over. Just for fun. They've never been here before. Never. Want an empanada?"

Robyn stood where she was, a quivering Sundae in her arms. She kept her eyes on Mrs. Zazueta, remembering what Jonathan had told them during their first class: Don't tell Nestor's parents. Don't tell Nestor's grandma. She had known not to ask why, and she had known to put the whole thing out of her head, and she had. But now here they were, the truth of things squarely in front of them.

Mrs. Zazueta took a few steps forward and pointed at Robyn. "I remember you." Then she pointed at Robyn's dogs. "I remember your dogs."

She made a clicking sound and the poodles trotted back inside the house. Her eyes narrowed, and she walked slowly across the lawn. She moved first to William and Tiger over at the tunnel. Then she crossed in front of Sundae and Robyn. Finally, she made her way to Nestor, Jonathan, and Alejandra. Their faces had turned pale, and they stared down at the grass. Fudge was by Alejandra's side, sniffing at the stinky treat that dangled from the end of the long barbecue tongs.

Mrs. Zazueta pointed at the treat. "Those are my treats. From my house."

Nestor nervously pushed back his cuticles with his thumbnail.

She pointed at Fudge. "This is the dog who is deaf and blind."

"She can see a little," said Robyn.

Swiftly, Mrs. Zazueta turned back to look at Robyn. Then she returned her gaze to Nestor. "You're teaching your own agility class? What makes you think—"

Nestor cut her off. "It's not agility training, Abuela. It's *ability* training. We invented it. Any dog can do it. You should see—"

She waved at Sundae and Fudge. "You heard me say that those dogs shouldn't learn agility."

"Technically, it's not agility, and it's very safe—"

"You're not a dog trainer, Nestor. You don't know what is safe." She turned and looked at Robyn. "And you. I told you no. Don't you care about your dogs at all?"

If there were ever a time to *not* go looking for trouble, this was it. This was Nestor's problem, and Robyn needed to let Nestor handle it.

Then again, whatever she felt about the people standing there, whatever they felt about her, she could not let Mrs. Zazueta get away with saying that she didn't care about her dogs. She loved Sundae and Fudge with her whole heart. And ability training *was* safe. That was the whole reason they were doing ability training. Because it was safer than agility training.

Without her meaning to, without her knowing how to stop it, Robyn's tongue decided to take a stand. "You did tell me no," she said. "But your husband knew, and he thought it was okay. And maybe Nestor's not an official dog trainer, but he is your assistant sometimes, and he was the youngest dog handler to compete in that one agility competition. And he's been doing a really good job, and he was just trying to save his parents some money, and I think . . ." She let her voice trail off as Mrs. Zazueta, her torso stretching, turned back to Nestor.

"You're my assistant now?" said Mrs. Zazueta. "And you're a competitive agility dog handler? And your grandfather said this was okay?"

From behind the glass door Robyn caught sight of Mr. Zazueta scurrying away from the window.

Jonathan had snuck over to Robyn. He whispered, "Thanks a lot, Robyn. Now you've really messed things up."

Mrs. Zazueta pointed her finger at Nestor. "I want everyone out. Now." She turned around, stomped into her house, and closed the door.

Robyn looked around. Jonathan wasn't the only one who looked angry at her—everyone did.

She got it. She had fought fire with fire. She had stood up for herself and her dogs. And somehow, despite herself, she had burned it all down.

Sighing, she leashed up her dogs. When she met Nivien outside the gate, she didn't say a word, even as Nivien frowned and draped an arm around her shoulder.

"You okay?" said Nivien.

"Yeah," she said softly. But, really, she was swimming in the pity pool. Why did she always manage to burn it all down?

CHAPTER 12

THE TRUTH CAME OUT in dribs and drabs.

"Robyn," said Jonathan with a scowl when he saw her entering the school. "You weren't supposed to say anything about Grandpa Z. Man-oh-man, is he in the doghouse now."

"I'm sorry. Okay?" she said, her expression defiant. She never could stay in the pity pool all that long, especially when there was blame to share. "It just came out. I didn't mean to get him in trouble." She put her hands on her hips. "Maybe you guys should have told her—told Nestor's whole family—what we were doing. Maybe it's your fault for not being honest."

Jonathan threw his arms in the air. "Grandpa Z. was the one who told us not to tell her. He knew she'd get mad. She's super protective of every dog she sees. She wouldn't believe we could do it. But we could. Obviously. We can."

He calmed down a little and looked away. "And we just didn't want Nestor's parents to worry about the math stuff. They worry all the time. They worry about everything."

Then a little more came out at lunch recess. Robyn was walking the blacktop with Marshan and Lulu. She was keeping her eyes on the pavement, eager to stay clear of Nestor, Jonathan, and Alejandra.

Lulu and Marshan were showing off the scratches they'd earned by dressing their cats in their latest sewing-class creations. Lulu had three long red marks on her left arm. Marshan had two on her right arm and one short one on her neck.

Robyn looked up. Jonathan was standing in the handball line, looking right at her. Nestor was playing Alejandra. Behind Jonathan stood Harrison. His feet were planted wide, and his snake eyes were roving all around. She didn't believe a word Jonathan, Alejandra, or anyone said. That kid was trouble.

Jonathan ran up to her. He said, "Come here."

She said, "Why?"

He frowned and motioned to her with his arms. "Over here."

Marshan and Lulu were watching with bright, curious eyes as she walked over to him.

"What?" she said.

He looked over at Marshan and Lulu. He stepped

a few feet farther away from them and made Robyn join him.

When he was sure no one was listening, he said to her, "Okay. I just want you to know that we didn't lie to you. Nestor *is* the youngest person to ever compete in a California Canine Club agility contest. It was last year."

"Okay," she said, not seeing why he couldn't have said any of that in front of Lulu and Marshan.

"But . . . the part I didn't tell you was that he only competed because Grandma Z. had to have emergency gallbladder surgery, and she had Nestor fill in for her so that Gigante could have his turn in the ring. She didn't want Gigante to miss out."

"Okay," she said again.

His brows were scrunched together, and his tongue peeked out from the side of his mouth. "And one more thing. We never said Nestor was Grandma Z.'s assistant. You thought that on your own. He just helps her set things up at the park sometimes, when Grandpa Z. can't."

"Well," she said awkwardly. "I'm sorry if I got you guys in trouble. I didn't mean to."

He waved her words away. "It's not that. I just don't want you talking about all this to Lulu and Marshan. They'll think Nestor was lying. But he wasn't. So don't say anything."

Robyn screwed up her face. "I won't, but I'm sure they won't think that."

He looked at them. "They will, and they'll be all, 'Poor, poor Nestor. He had cancer. Blah, blah, blah. And now he's making up stories.'"

He shot her a warning look. "You really should have kept your mouth shut, Robyn." Then he ran back to the handball line.

"Wait," she said.

He turned around.

"So . . . is that it? No more ability training." She felt the finality of her words, the end they represented not just to the work she was doing with Sundae and Fudge, but to the friendship she might still have been able to build with Alejandra, Nestor, and Jonathan.

A run of emotions crossed Jonathan's face. "We're working on it." And with that, he was gone.

Robyn walked glumly back to Lulu and Marshan, who looked at her expectantly.

Robyn shrugged. "Just dog-training stuff."

They walked a little more, none of them speaking, the three of them just looking around.

Lulu sighed. "Poor Nestor. He's such a sad case."

She seemed to be waiting for Robyn to say something. But Robyn let the silence between them hang. Now that she thought about it, maybe Lulu and Marshan could be a little bit gossipy. But was that so bad?

Lots of people were gossipy. Maybe most people. That went hand in hand with being judgey.

She looked over at the handball wall. Alejandra was playing Harrison.

Lulu and Marshan had changed topics. Now they were talking about the sewing machines in their sewing class. They were ranking them from most clunky and annoying to least.

Alejandra slammed the ball against the handball wall. Harrison ran toward it, but it bounced a second time, and he scowled and let out a loud groan.

"Mooove," shouted Nestor. "You're out."

Jonathan and Alejandra started to laugh.

Nestor was doing what he always did. He was trying not to smile and only slightly succeeding. He glanced up and caught Robyn's eye, and there it was: the smile. No teeth but a definite arch to the mouth. He turned sideways and tried to hide it.

She smiled a little herself. Then she sighed. Maybe it would have been better if she had never made that list of stupid rules.

CHAPTER 13

HOPE!

It arrived that weekend.

Robyn and Mom were at the dog beach when Alejandra texted: Ability training is back on. Nestor will explain when we go to his house.

Robyn let out a squeal.

Mom pointed at her. "What did I tell you? The dog beach is a no-phone zone. Hand it over."

Robyn handed Mom her phone, but she didn't care. Ability training was back on, and Alejandra was texting her about it, which meant she wasn't banned forever and they probably weren't mad at her anymore. And if they weren't mad at her anymore, maybe she still had a chance to be real friends with them, the kind of friend that mattered even more than a full-size candy bar.

"What was that about anyway?" asked Mom.

Robyn had been too embarrassed to tell Mom about

what had happened with Mrs. Zazueta. She just said, "Dog-training stuff."

"You're really liking that, aren't you?"

"I love it. It's going great," said Robyn. Then she ran down to the water's edge to watch Sundae and Fudge bark at waves.

She was all ready for the next ability class. Halloween was behind her. Mrs. Zazueta's outrage was behind her. It was all good. It was better than good. It was great. Because she'd thought of a way to draw all the good snack attention back to herself. She wouldn't even try to compete with restaurant empanadas. Really, who could? Instead, she'd mix things up by bringing the best drink ever: hot chocolate with mini-marshmallows. She was going to fill a whole thermos with it. Then people could have both things, and they would say, "Wow! How have we not thought of adding a delightful drink to snack time until today? Thank you, Robyn, for your important contribution, which is just as good a contribution as anyone else is making."

But then it began to rain. And it didn't stop raining for two weeks. So there was no ability class. There wasn't even recess. There was only sit and eat with your seat mates, and then play Connect 4 or checkers at your desk. Except Lulu didn't like Connect 4, and Marshan didn't like checkers. And Robyn did not like to take sides by choosing, which Lulu and Marshan insisted she do. It was an unwinnable situation. No matter what she chose, someone snipped and snapped at her.

The rains stopped, but then it was Thanksgiving break. And Nestor's family was off to visit relatives in Santa Cruz. So there was no ability class.

And once school resumed, the rains returned. And there were more disagreements between Marshan and Lulu over Connect 4 and Checkers. So no more ability class. No more recess.

And just when the weather dried out, it was winter break. Robyn always spent the holidays with Dad, so she flew to Toronto the day after school ended. She returned after New Year's, happy to be reunited with Mom and the wildly delighted Sundae and Fudge.

She was also excited to restart ability training. Dad had taken her and Joshua to a dog show in Toronto, where she'd seen an amazing demonstration of scent-tracking dogs. The demonstration had given her a few ideas on how to better help not just Fudge, but Sundae, Tiger, and even Bruce, especially with the weave poles. But ideas weren't the only things she brought back from Canada. She also came home with a bad cold that turned out to be strep throat. So Robyn once more missed ability class.

But one good thing happened. Marshan and Lulu really proved their mettle. Every day that she was sick, they brought her her homework and sat with her for a few minutes, filling her in on the who, the what, and the why.

"Mrs. Wang got so mad at Harrison," they said one day.

"Some kid in the other fifth-grade class threw up all over the lunch tables," they said another.

And Robyn realized that you've got to give it to gossip sniffers. At least they help you know what's going on.

When she returned to school, they were just as supportive.

"You've been sick. You choose what we do at lunch recess," Marshan said to her.

"Handball!" Robyn said excitedly.

Lulu's and Marshan's faces fell.

"Or . . . basketball?" tried Robyn.

Basketball it was. They played it for two straight days. And the next day they played tetherball.

Boom. She beat Marshan.

Boom. She beat Lulu.

Boom. There was one more person in line. Nestor.

Lulu and Marshan looked at her, and Robyn could see two things.

1. They did not like it that she'd beaten them so
   easily.
2. Tetherball time was over. It was time to walk
   away.

"Um," she said. "It would be mean to leave Nestor with no one to play against . . . "

They blinked their surprise.

"Okay," said Lulu, stretching out the word.

"Suit yourself," said Marshan. She linked arms with Lulu and the two of them sauntered away, their heads bent toward each other, their mouths moving fast.

She looked at Nestor, and—boom—she beat him.

"Tetherball is lame," he mumbled. "You should come back and play handball some time."

There it was again—hope. "Okay." She smiled. "I will."

But once she returned to the classroom, Marshan and Lulu put their feet down.

"It was kind of harsh of you to keep playing tetherball with Nestor even when Lulu and I were done. I mean, we only played because of you. It's only right that you should have stopped when we were ready to stop," said Marshan as they were settling back into their seats.

"Same as basketball. We don't even like basketball. We just did it to be nice," said Lulu. "And we brought you your homework all those days."

"And, for a long time, we made sure that Harrison didn't bother you. We've been, like, really good to you."

"It's not so much that," said Lulu. "But it would have been nicer for you to think of our feelings this time."

"Oh," said Robyn, a deer-in-the-headlights blankness turning her face an unnatural shade of gray.

"You know what else?" Lulu said, whispering now because Mrs. Wang had told them to get out their books for silent reading. "Seeing Nestor? It reminded me. You said we could come see your dog-training class sometime. And you never did invite us."

Robyn, who had never said that she wanted them to come to ability training, who had until very recently wanted to keep the worlds of ability training and school separate, bit her tongue. Then, stumbling over her words, she tried to explain that she herself had not been to the class in weeks.

Marshan shook her head. "You also said you'd find out why Alejandra wears purple. She does the dog training with you. You could ask her anytime."

Well, here Robyn could at least defend herself, however carefully. "I did," she told them. "She got mad at me. I'm sorry. I really did try."

Lulu and Marshan sighed and frowned as they opened their books.

That was it. She hadn't worked this hard to blend

in with Marshan and Lulu just to lose them over a tetherball game. "I'm sorry. You're right. I shouldn't have played that extra game of tetherball. We were doing it together. When you were done, I should have been done."

They nodded, their eyes still on their books.

"And," she said, ready to make this work, "I'll talk to Nestor. Of course you can come to my dog-training class."

Prim little smiles pulled up their mouths, but they still looked at their books.

"And . . . I'll actually just talk to Alejandra . . . right now . . . and she can tell Nestor."

They looked up, suddenly interested.

Lulu glanced at Mrs. Wang and then back at Robyn. She mouthed the word "Okay."

Robyn swallowed hard, and when Mrs. Wang called another student to her desk, Robyn snuck over to Alejandra.

But she couldn't just jump right into telling her about Lulu and Marshan. First, she had to warm things up. "I can finally go to ability tomorrow."

"Oh, good," said Alejandra, sounding genuinely happy. "Wait until you see. We have some surprises for you."

"Okay," said Robyn. She glanced at Lulu and Marshan. "Um . . . I'll meet you at the gate after school.

Sundae and Fudge will be happy to see you when we pick them up."

Alejandra blinked. "Oh. Sorry. I've been walking with Nestor and Jonathan. I help them set things up now."

Harrison looked over at Robyn. "Why are your dogs named after dessert?"

Robyn had always liked the names Sundae and Fudge. She thought they were cute and that they got straight at the heart of the dogs' close bond. But she had the feeling that Harrison didn't care about any of that. He was just trying to get under her skin, make her think there was something wrong with her and Mom for choosing such sweet names.

But she'd been in school for half a year by now. She still considered herself a new kid compared to everyone else, but she wasn't a first-week newbie either. And this time she was ready to make her stand.

She said, "Because I like those names. Why are your eyes beady like a snake's?"

Alejandra let out a soft moan. "That was mean, Robyn."

Harrison's head fell forward. "Yeah. That hurt my feelings."

Alejandra patted Harrison's shoulder. "You just have regular eyes, Harrison. Don't worry."

"Robyn, go back to your seat," said Mrs. Wang out of nowhere.

Without a word, Robyn slunk to her desk.

Marshan and Lulu looked up from their work.

"I didn't get a chance to tell her," Robyn whispered. "But it's okay. You can come next week. Yeah. I'm sure it's fine if you come next week."

Lulu and Marshan squeezed each other's hands. They looked at each other in excitement. Then they turned to her.

Marshan said, "And it's okay about the tetherball. But let's not play things like that anymore. They cause too much trouble."

"Marshan's right," said Lulu. "And tetherball is kind of stupid, if you think about it. I mean what's the point?"

Marshan nodded. "What's the point."

Robyn actually kind of liked tetherball. She liked pounding the ball with all her might and watching it spin around the pole. But she nodded anyway. "Exactly. What's the point?"

She felt her whole body relax. Phew, crisis averted. Finally, things were good. She had been tested, which was maybe only fair, and she had survived. But things were also super clear now too. She could spend her free time in school doing what she wanted, like playing handball or tetherball and maybe getting closer to Nestor, Alejandra, and Jonathan, or she could maintain the peace with Lulu and Marshan. The two people who'd looked out for her. The two blender-inners she'd blended in with so well. But she couldn't do both. The first choice offered a possibility of fun and new friendship, but also, eyeballs on her back and judgment to her face. The second choice offered proven friendship and the safety of the potted and overlooked plant. Plus, hadn't Lulu and Marshan made it abundantly clear? She owed them. Boy, did she owe them.

It was a lot to puzzle over: what she owed others versus what she owed herself, what she wanted versus what was safe. She thought about these questions so much that it took her a few days before she asked herself another question: Why did Nestor and Jonathan suddenly need Alejandra's help setting up for the ability class? What had there ever been to set up in the first place?

CHAPTER 14

ROBYN LISTENED TO THE sound of Sundae's and Fudge's nails as they tapped against the sidewalk. She could tell by their eager clicking and clacking—all energy and anticipation—that her dogs were as excited to return to ability training as she was.

But she couldn't lie. She was nervous too. Because—ugh—she was going to have to tell Nestor that she'd be bringing Marshan and Lulu next week, and who knew what he'd think about that? Plus—she couldn't stop thinking about it—why *did* Nestor and Jonathan suddenly need Alejandra's help in setting up? And what about William? Had they asked him for help? She could have helped. She would have been happy to help.

Nivien kept trying to make conversation—asking about her day, asking about her homework. Honestly, it only made Robyn more nervous. It was just another voice making it hard for her to concentrate.

It made her feel weighed down. And she already had literal reason to feel weighed down. In addition to her math book, her backpack contained a thermos of hot chocolate, a bag of mini-marshmallows, and—for good measure—a canister of whipped cream.

From down the street she spied Mrs. Zazueta's yard. It was already decorated for Valentine's Day, with a giant blow-up bear holding what looked like a greeting card. From the trees hung shiny red hearts, and on the door a pink cupid held a bow. As Robyn approached the gate to the backyard, she could hear what sounded like a party in Nestor's backyard.

She looked at Nivien, who shrugged. She went to Nestor's gate. She knocked.

No one answered.

She knocked again.

Still no one answered.

She knocked a third time.

The gate opened, and there was a rushed-looking Nestor, who barely looked at her. He just ushered her in, locked the gate behind her, and then ran off toward the outdoor dining table, where Jonathan, Alejandra, William, and William's dog, Tiger, stood milling around.

There were also four new kids and four new dogs. All of them—dogs and people—were acting like they'd known each other forever. Two of the kids she didn't recognize. They were on the tall side, though, and they were talking to William, so she thought maybe they went to the middle school with him. One of them had a pug and the other had a pit bull. Both dogs seemed as old as Moses.

The two other kids she did recognize. One was Nestor's friend, the one who wore glasses and used arm braces. She had with her an enormous, glossy-coated German shepherd. It looked like it could eat Fudge in three bites and Sundae in four. As for the fourth kid, she could not believe her eyes. It was Harrison. Harrison! He stood near a rust-colored dachshund. Out of nowhere, the dachshund keeled over and started to nap.

She glanced over at the poodles watching from behind the sliding glass door. Their eyes were narrow, their gazes intense, like maybe they were deciding whose head to sit on next. And that seemed weird too. Shouldn't they have been growling and scratching at the glass, trying desperately to get at these invaders?

Jonathan came up to her. He was carrying a clipboard. "Checking in with Sundae and Fudge?"

Her chin fell forward.

He took it as a nod and said, "Go ahead and unleash your dogs. We like to start with dog socialization time."

If she had just run across a Martian, her expression

would not have been more shocked. She bent down, unhooked the leashes. She stood back up. "Dog socialization time? What about math?"

He looked at her like a waiter about to share the sad news that they'd run out of the daily special. "Oh," he said, stretching out the word. "Didn't anyone tell you? We don't do that anymore. Nestor's parents got him a real tutor. When Grandma Z. told Nestor's parents how Nestor and I were exchanging math lessons for ability classes, they were all, 'If you need help, you're seeing an expert.' Now we both go to Kumon." He sighed. "It's way less fun."

Robyn was watching her dogs. Fudge's nose was right up in the German shepherd's butt. Sundae stood a way back and was sniffing from afar.

Confused, Robyn said to Jonathan, "But I thought you said real tutors were too expensive."

Jonathan shrugged. "I guess they're making it work. They know that a Nobel Prize isn't gonna jump into Nestor's lap."

He readjusted his clipboard and put his pencil in his shirt pocket. "Anyway, now we just do ability dog training (Trademark Nestor Zazueta). We start with dog socialization. Grandma Z. says it's very important when you're working with a group this size, and even though she's teaching her own classes, she's also sort of overseeing Nestor's class. She says if he's going to do this, he's gotta do it right. And she's gonna make sure he does."

"You mean . . ." Robyn glanced around. "All these people are in the class now? Since when?"

William suddenly appeared at the outdoor dining table with a tray of little toasts and a bowl of something that smelled of garlic, basil, and tomatoes.

"Yum," said Jonathan, excitement lighting up his eyes. "Bruschetta."

Weasels could not have moved faster than the group of people clamoring to get at that tray. Even Nestor's grandpa was suddenly out of his house and racing toward them. He walked right past her, banging his elbow against her backpack.

It reminded her. "Oh," she said, unzipping the bag. "I should put this on the table."

"Is that hot chocolate?" asked Jonathan as she pulled out the thermos and whipped cream.

Robyn smiled and nodded. Here it came: a taste of the appreciation she desired and deserved.

But Jonathan made his sad waiter face again. "Sorry. Grandma Z. says if we are going to do this like it's a real sport, we have to eat like real athletes. No junk food. We can't even do the empanadas. Grandma Z. says they're too greasy. But William's parents are on top of it. They put something together for us every week. They did the bruschetta before. It's really good." He waited a beat and then jogged toward the table, saying, "I'm gonna get me some."

She was holding her breath. So Jonathan—*Jonathan!*—was saying she couldn't put out her hot chocolate? And she couldn't put out her mini-marshmallows or whipped cream? It was *whipped cream*! Food of the gods!

She looked more closely at the new people. The girl with glasses and arm braces was talking to Alejandra. Robyn couldn't hear them. They were on the far side of the table, and there were so many people chitchatting away.

Robyn sighed. She watched Jonathan scoop some of the tomato mixture onto the bread and then strut over to Mrs. Zazueta's glass door. He stood with his food in front of Bruce.

She went over to him.

He took a bite of the bruschetta. "Sometimes, I like to show them who's boss."

Across the glass, Bruce squinted. His mouth twitched.

"Try all you want," Jonathan said to the dog. "You're not getting any of this. I double-checked that door myself."

Of all the people involved with Nestor's dog-training

class, Robyn felt like she understood Jonathan the most. He was like her. They were practical, logical people who saw the world for what it was. So when she bored her eyes into his and said, "But . . . why?" she knew he would understand.

He put the final bite of bruschetta in his mouth and transferred the juice of the tomatoes from his hands onto his pants. He swallowed and licked his lips.

He told her that on the day Grandma Z. had found them all in the yard, she had seen a lot more than she let on. She saw even more when she cooled down and Grandpa Z. convinced her to give Nestor and Jonathan a chance, to let them show her what they were doing and how ability worked. So they did. They brought out Bruce. They ran him through the tunnel and through the tire jump. Then they showed how they spotted him on the A-frame.

That had done the trick. Grandma Z. wasn't just impressed. She was proud of Nestor and Jonathan. And she wasn't just proud of the training program. She was also proud of how they'd tried to solve their math struggles by themselves and—most importantly—of what they were creating.

"Which didn't mean we weren't in trouble," said Jonathan. "Because she was *way* mad at us and Grandpa Z. for keeping her in the dark." He shrugged. "But Grandma Z. blows up big and cools down fast.

"The point is," he said, looking back at the table, "finally, Grandma Z. stepped in and now"—he held up the clipboard—"we're super organized and professional."

Robyn looked again across the yard at all the people, all the pets. So this was ability now. No math. No junk food. Just a regular, organized, professional class. With clipboards, a teacher, assistants, a healthy snack, and . . . what? What did everyone else get to contribute? Because contributions made things equal. Contributions made everyone important.

Jonathan almost seemed to read her mind. His shoulders fell forward, and he said, "I said if it's a real class it should cost real money, but Grandma Z. said no way because Nestor's just a kid. Personally, I don't think she wants the competition."

Jonathan frowned. He motioned toward the little dachshund, who had fallen asleep again. This time with its head on the ground and its back legs on top of the old pug.

"Harrison," he called, pointing to the dog.

Harrison rushed over to his dog and slid its back legs onto the grass.

"Strudel's always falling asleep in the weirdest places and ways. It'd be sort of funny if it weren't some awful sickness."

"Strudel?" said Robyn, remembering how Harrison

had asked about her dogs' names. "Isn't that a dessert?"

Jonathan shook his head. "I don't know. But she's an ability demon, although one time she did fall asleep in the tunnel and we couldn't get her out for a long time." He motioned to the yardful of dogs. "Actually, they're all good. They can do the tunnel, the tire jump, and the hurdle. Today we're starting them on the dog walk."

Robyn had been doing okay with all of this. And it was a *lot* to have to be okay with. She understood what had happened. She understood how the class had changed and why. It killed her a little, but she was being flexible (rule number ten), and she even understood why she couldn't serve her delicious hot chocolate. And she accepted, although with some annoyance toward him but none toward his adorable dog, that Harrison was now a member of the class. But something had shifted inside her. "But . . . what about my dogs? They're way past the dog walk."

Her eyes scanned the yard again in search of Fudge and Sundae. She saw them sitting next to Alejandra, who was doling out ear scratches: German shepherd, Fudge, Sundae; German shepherd, Fudge, Sundae.

"Didn't Alejandra tell you?" asked Jonathan. "Alejandra," he called.

When she ran over, he said, "Didn't you tell Robyn about Sundae and Fudge?"

Alejandra beamed. "I told her we had some surprises!" She turned to Robyn. "Surprise! Grandma Z. wants Sundae to join her intermediate agility class."

It took a minute for the news to sink in. "What?" said Robyn.

"She saw him doing the course," said Alejandra. "That day she got mad at us. She saw Sundae. She thinks he's a natural and that, with the right training, he could be a champion."

Nestor came and stood next to them.

"And get this," said Jonathan. "She thinks you're a natural too. A born dog handler. And she would know."

Robyn was a born handler? Sundae was a born champion? A spark ignited inside her. It was, somehow, just what she'd always known, what she'd felt the first time she laid eyes on Mrs. Zazueta's class. That she and her dogs were supposed to do agility.

"Wait," she said suddenly. "No. It won't work. Sundae's okay training here, with Fudge nearby, but he wouldn't want to do a whole class without her. And what would Fudge do? Just sit home, alone? That's not fair."

"We told Grandma Z. that," said Jonathan. "She thinks they're ready for the challenge."

"And the best part," said Alejandra, "is that you don't need to worry about Fudge. Grandma Z.'s intermediate class is at the same time as ours. So you can drop off Fudge here, go to the park, and pick Fudge up after you're done. So she'll still have plenty of fun."

Nestor said, "Fudge knows a lot. She'll be our demonstration dog."

Robyn had been nodding steadily along, thinking about it, imagining it. But now she stopped nodding. "You're going to make Fudge your demonstration dog," she repeated. Her voice was flat. They had already decided all of this, which meant that they had all been planning it, and talking about it, and just taking for granted that they could decide what she would do.

"Yeah," said Jonathan. "We thought Fudge could be our Gigante."

"You should do it." Nestor was looking at her blankly while Jonathan—and now Alejandra—looked at her with bright shoe-salespeople smiles.

Robyn knew in her gut that there was more going on here than they were saying. Something about their whole story smelled bad, and it wasn't just that Robyn had stepped in dog poop, which she had. No. She believed the part about Mrs. Zazueta wanting her and Sundae to join her class. It would be impossible to lie about something like that. But she also believed that they were happy to see her go. Why else plan it all out without ever telling her a word?

She felt a tingling behind her eyes.

"Isn't it a great surprise?" said Alejandra, sounding pleased but also, maybe, a little *too* pleased. "This way, you can be with us one last time, and you can start with Grandma Z. next week."

"She's not your grandma," snapped Robyn.

A flash of hurt crossed Alejandra's face. "She's not Jonathan's grandma either. She says it's okay to call her that."

Robyn flushed. Everyone was best friends with Grandma Z. now. Everyone was best friends with one another, and they were all so fine with all the changes that had happened. They were being so *flexible*, so flexible, in fact, that they'd just moved on. They'd just left her behind. Like she'd never existed. Like what had happened so many times before.

CHAPTER 15

ROBYN KNEW THAT THERE were three phases to being a professional-level new kid. Phase one: the excluded period. During this phase, the new kid—in this case Robyn—would be excluded.

People didn't usually exclude her to be mean. She understood that. People excluded her because they already knew a lot of people, and she was not one of them. During this phase, all she could do was wait it out. She'd thought the rules would help. She'd thought the rules would draw the right attention to her so that, eventually, people *would* get to know her and even like her.

Phase two: the blended-in period. This was the dream. This was when Robyn felt like she'd blended into the fabric of her new world. By this time, which varied due to a million different things that could never be predicted, she had been somewhere long enough to be considered a classmate or friend, as opposed to a *new* classmate or friend.

This was where Robyn found herself with Lulu and Marshan. Blended in. True. It was not a perfect friendship. They didn't share that many interests. She could sometimes feel pulled between them. She could sometimes feel judged by them. But she had wanted to blend in with them. And, half a year into the school year, she had.

But there is also phase three of being a new kid: the forgetting period. This is the period when Robyn would move somewhere new and find herself almost instantly erased from the memories of all the people she had finally blended in with. At least it seemed that way. Friends would promise to stay in touch. But they never did, at least not for long. Because here is the truth, or at least how Robyn understood it: out of sight, out of mind. If you aren't there to show people you exist, they will forget you entirely.

Phase one. Phase two. Phase three. That's the order. Every time. As predictable as moving itself.

So what the hecky-heck heck? Robyn was still working toward phase two with Alejandra, Nestor, and Jonathan, and already they were phase-threeing her.

She realized it that night. She was lying with Sundae and Fudge in bed. She was trying to get to sleep, trying not to remember Nestor's blank face when he said, "You should do it."

She thought back to Halloween, when she had spent all night waiting for them to come to her house. She had believed them when they said they'd forgotten and that they didn't think she would care. She had blamed herself for building a wall between them, for making herself less important to them than a candy bar. And she'd believed them again when they said, "Come back to ability. Come back to handball."

But they hadn't meant it. It had just been a lot of talk. They'd been giving her the phase three treatment all along. She meant nothing to them. It was the worst kind of rejection. A puncher or a name-caller at least sees you, has an opinion about you. A phase three rejection doesn't even care enough about you to do that. To be phase-three-ed is to be an ant to the elephant, a grain of sand to the wide beach. It is to be insignificant.

But Robyn knew she was not insignificant. The only reason the ability-training class existed was because of her! She knew that. Everyone knew that. Everything about that class had started with Robyn and her goal to teach Sundae and Fudge agility. She was the one who'd first believed that the non-Gigantes of the worlds could do dog obstacle courses. She, with her discovery of touch training, had been the one who had the first inkling that the task needed to fit the dog, not the dog the task.

And, sure, Nestor was the expert. He'd been in that fancy competition, even if only as a substitute. He knew all the obstacles and had helped train Gigante. And, yes, Alejandra and Jonathan—by helping Fudge—had become his assistants. But it had all started with *Robyn*. And *Robyn's* dogs. And *Robyn's* snacks.

Being made insignificant hurt. It physically hurt. It hurt her gut, her throat, her head. And experience had taught her that there was only one way to get over that pain. And that was to phase-three the rejectors right back. All those people in every city she'd ever lived in? She was done with them. She erased them right away, before they could erase her. So Alejandra, Nestor, and Jonathan? She would erase them too. They were nothing to her now. They were a three-person-size hole in her memory.

And as for the intermediate agility class with Mrs. Zazueta? Well, that was gone too. It was too bad. It was sad. But better to crush a dream than to have any reminders of how little she meant to any of them.

She told Mom the next day. They had just said goodbye to Nivien, and now Mom stood warming a bowl of lentil soup in the microwave.

As casual as could be, Robyn said, "I think I'm ready to move on from dog training. I'm ready to try something new."

Mom looked up at her. She was dressed in exercise clothes from a Zumba class she had just started at the university. She was taking it with some of the other biologists. She had a hawklike look on her face. "But you like dog training."

Robyn sat cross-legged on the kitchen floor and began to scratch Fudge.

Sundae came over and tried to horn in. Fudge nosed him hard in his chest, and he settled himself at Robyn's feet.

Robyn explained things just like she'd planned. "Yeah, but Marshan and Lulu are taking sewing. If I take it too, I could learn to make clothes for Sundae and Fudge. Wouldn't that be cute?"

Mom stirred the soup. "Just do both. Your grandma Kellen loves to sew. She'll be so excited to see what you make."

Robyn tensed her shoulders. "I just want to do one after-school activity."

Mom turned to the refrigerator and took out some broccoli. "Why do one fun thing when you can do two? I think you can handle it."

"I just want to do sewing," said Robyn firmly.

Mom made a funny sound. She pulled out a chopping board and started slicing the broccoli. "I wonder if the dog training is starting to get hard."

"No," said Robyn. "I'm just . . . I want to try

something new. You like me to try new things."

"You know, I was reading this book about teaching." Mom tried to make it sound like she had just remembered this book out of nowhere, like she was launching into a random new conversation.

Robyn knew better.

"It said that we need to have *growth mind-sets.*"

Snorty-snort-snort-snort. Robyn rolled her eyes, thinking that this conversation was why no one should have to grow up with a teacher for a parent.

"We have to believe that we can get better, that we can get past challenges. The difference between 'I can't' and 'I can't *yet*' can make all the difference in the world."

Robyn raised her arms and dropped them in frustration. "I'm tired of dog training."

"Just think about it," said Mom. She looked over at Sundae and Fudge. "If not for you, for them."

Robyn collapsed forward. Her forehead tapped against Fudge's, and Fudge's warm dog breath filled her nose. Of all the dirty tricks in the world: making her think of Sundae and Fudge, of how much they liked their training, how much they'd grown from it.

Pressure began to build behind her eyes. Worried that she might cry, she lifted Fudge off her and turned farther away from Mom.

Mom sat down next to her. "What's wrong?"

Robyn's lower lip began to tremble. She pulled her head up. Haltingly, she explained what had happened in Nestor's class during her long absence and how, now, everyone was so excited for her and Sundae to leave so that they could just keep working with Fudge all by themselves.

Mom's eyes started to glisten, as if she too might cry, which only made Robyn feel even closer to crying.

"Oh, honey," said Mom with unexpected sweetness. "I think you're seeing this all wrong. It sounds like they're just excited for you and that they see training Fudge as a way to keep you connected."

"No," said Robyn. "It's just like Halloween. They don't care about me. They like it better when I'm not there."

"I don't think so," Mom said. "You know what I think? I think that all of you have given Sundae and Fudge an amazing gift. You and your friends have taught our sweet pooches so much confidence and strength. I've seen it at home. I may not talk about it a lot, but I have. I've been so impressed. But now Sundae and Fudge are ready to spread their wings and try something apart from each other. It's incredible. After all they've been through. Well done. And well done to your friends. You should be proud of yourselves."

Robyn got up and moved to a kitchen chair. She

told herself that Mom didn't understand at all, and that was all it took. The tears burst forth.

Mom followed her to the table. She squeezed Robyn's hand. "And do you know the best part? Now you can do what you really wanted. You can learn *real* agility training from a *real* expert in a *real* class. Can you believe it? Our nervous little Sundae? Taking intermediate agility? Maybe I can come watch sometime, and I can meet your friends when we drop off Fudge. I would like that."

A bubble of anger popped inside Robyn. "They're not my friends. They were never my friends. It was a bargain we made."

Mom tilted her head, looked at her thoughtfully. "I'd still like to meet them. They seem like interesting people who do interesting things. You know?"

CHAPTER 16

MOM WON THE BATTLE. She was not letting Robyn quit anything. When they were halfway through dinner—after Robyn had insisted and insisted and insisted that she wasn't doing anything that was remotely connected to Alejandra, Nestor, and Jonathan—Mom dropped the hammer.

"You're doing the intermediate agility class, and Fudge is doing the ability class," she said. "You said Mrs. Zazueta called you and Sundae naturals. That kind of compliment doesn't get tossed around every day. Mrs. Zazueta sees something special in both of you. You have to at least give it a try."

Robyn muttered that she was going to tell Dad how mean Mom was being.

And maybe that was the wrong response. Because that set Mom on a roll.

"I blame myself," she said, dropping her spoon and pushing away her soup bowl. "I should have been emphasizing the value of persistence. When you start something, you finish it. But we were moving a lot, and finding new activities was sometimes easier than finding ones you'd tried before. I told you. We're here for the long haul. So now you're going to lean into the hard stuff, even if it makes you a little uncomfortable."

"A lot uncomfortable," growled Robyn.

Mom got up from the table and started to clean the kitchen, abandoning her meal completely. "This will be a good opportunity for you, and it will be good for the dogs. And, for at least the first time, I'm taking you there myself."

Fine. Whatever. Even if she did have to take intermediate agility with Mrs. Zazueta, and even if Fudge did have to continue ability training without her own owner being present, Robyn would still find a way to phase-three Alejandra, Nestor, and Jonathan better than they phase-three-ed her. And she would start at the one place Mom couldn't boss her: school.

This was the rule she made herself: She would not talk to Alejandra, Nestor, or Jonathan. She would not look at them. She would not acknowledge them in any way. They were erased from her life, completely erased.

But dang it! As much as she tried to erase them, they kept popping up in front of her eyeballs.

There was Alejandra, waving her purple-sleeved arm every time the teacher asked a question, flitting around the classroom and helping people with math, volunteering to empty the trash or clean the dry-erase boards, snapping at anyone who whispered "Grape."

Alejandra specifically talked to Robyn too. That very next morning, she said, "Are you excited about intermediate agility?"

"Ehm," mumbled Robyn, not looking up from her work.

Alejandra refused to realize what was happening. She whispered back, "Oh, you're still working on your reading. Sorry." Then she tiptoed away.

Lunch was even worse. Robyn had positioned herself very strategically so that she would not have to see the faces of Alejandra, Nestor, Jonathan, or now, also, Harrison, and the girl who used arm braces and wore glasses. She didn't want to see any of them. They'd all formed a big group now. They were a regular pack, all the ability people who went to her school but her.

And then there they were, back together after they'd left their table. Alejandra, the other girl, and Jonathan were sitting on the bench near the water fountain. Nestor and Harrison stood in front of them. Nestor was rattling away, his arms moving up and down, in and out, while he spoke. He had never spoken like that when she was around.

Robyn had finished her food, but Lulu and Marshan were nibbling as slowly as ever.

Robyn saw the happy pack smile at Nestor, as if they were all about to start laughing.

"Erase, erase, erase," Robyn told herself.

But at the same time, she also couldn't help thinking, *What in the world is Nestor yakking about?*

Quick as could be, she corrected herself. *No. Who cares? Erase, erase, erase.*

Lulu and Marshan were talking about what they should do next.

Robyn focused on that. She turned sideways. "More basketball?" she said hopefully.

Marshan rested her elbow on the table and dropped her head onto her palm. "Too sweaty."

So now it was down to these two options: they could walk around the blacktop, or they could do something wild and *sit* on the blacktop.

"You can't sit on the blacktop," said Robyn, remembering—with a twinge of sadness—how the yard duty assistant had told Alejandra to get up when she had fallen to the ground laughing.

"Well, then let's just walk around," said Lulu.

Marshan had a glint in her eye. She didn't want to get in trouble, but, at the same time, she thought it might be fun to see how the yard attendant handled it. She said, "I say we try. What do you think, Robyn?"

Robyn thought this was Connect 4 versus checkers all over again. "Hmmm," she said, trying to think of a third option that would not get either friend mad at her.

But then, there they were: the nonexistent nobodies, taking up all the space in her field of vision. This time they were in the handball line. Jonathan had somehow convinced a teacher or member of the office staff to lend him a swivel chair. The girl who used arm braces was sitting on it, and he was turning her in circles.

A lump formed in Robyn's throat. If she thought about it, wasn't it now also the ability people's fault that she couldn't run and go play handball right then and there? All those other times she hadn't played, it had been different. Then it was a choice. But now it wasn't a choice. Now, if she went to play handball, she'd have to deal with them. And she couldn't deal with them because she was ignoring them. So now she added stealing handball to their list of crimes.

She looked away from the handball line. Then she looked back again. Alejandra and the other girl were singing—loudly—while waiting for their turns. Robyn could hear them all the way from where she stood with Lulu and Marshan. Not just that. Alejandra was dancing in place, twisting her hips one way and then another. The whole world could have been watching her and it didn't seem like she would even care. She was dressed in purple tights, a purple dress, and a purple coat.

Robyn spat out, "That Alejandra is such a grape. And it's not just all the purple. She's annoying."

Lulu's eyes narrowed as she nodded along with Marshan. In a hungry voice, she said, "She needs to relax. She tries to be *so* nice, and she talks *so* much, but then she gets mad if you ask her why she only wears purple. It's not normal."

Robyn nodded. "It's not normal at all. And the way she skipped a grade? That wasn't normal either."

Marshan leaned in closer. "I always wonder if it has to do with her mom."

With piercing eyes, Robyn stared at Marshan. "What happened to her mom?"

"It's sad," said Lulu.

"Really sad," said Marshan. "The government made her leave the country."

It took a moment for those words to sink into Robyn's body. They made no sense. What did they mean?

She couldn't help it. She glanced again at Alejandra. She had stopped singing and dancing and now she was playing handball against the other girl, who was knocking the ball with one brace as Jonathan moved the swivel chair back and forth toward the ball.

Alejandra was smiling. She didn't look like someone whose mom had been kicked out of the country. It seemed to Robyn that something like that would hang off you like a cheap metal necklace that stained your neck green.

Marshan shrugged. "Her mom wasn't supposed to be here. That's what my mom said. She wasn't supposed to be here, so they kicked her out. Her brother too. He was in middle school with my brother. Isn't it sad?"

Robyn was still processing the news about Alejandra's mom, but she looked at Marshan because . . . what was it? Even though Marshan said it was sad, she didn't sound sad. She sounded almost gleeful.

"When was this?" asked Robyn. She still couldn't believe it. A mom should get to stay with their kid. That seemed like the most obvious thing in the world.

She hadn't even known Alejandra had a brother. Alejandra had never said one word about him. Come to think of it, she didn't talk about her mom either. She talked about her dad. She talked about Argentine school. She talked about many things, just not those two. It was like they didn't exist. Like they'd been erased.

"It was a few years ago," said Marshan. "I don't remember exactly. But that's why I wonder if maybe it's not her fault that she's annoying. Maybe she's the way she is because of what happened."

"Maybe," said Lulu. "But then that's extra sad, isn't it?"

It *was* sad. Everything about it was extra sad. And

it served like a Magic Marker, coloring Robyn's image of Alejandra in deeper, more complex colors, even as Robyn tried not to think of Alejandra at all. She wondered what Alejandra's face had looked like when her mom left. And had she known her mom would have to leave the country, or did she come home one day and—poof—no more mom? Would her mom ever come back? Did she still talk to her mom? Did they video chat like Robyn and Dad? Because a lot of people had phase-three-ed Robyn, but never Dad. Not once, Dad.

Robyn had moved, and moved on, from many things. But she wondered how someone could move on from something like that.

It suddenly occurred to Robyn that this kept happening. Out of the blue—out of nowhere—she'd hear these stories about people, people she thought she knew but apparently did not. It was another classic new-kid problem. Wherever she moved, everyone knew everyone else's backstory except her. In Portland, her whole class got angry at her for talking about Sundae and Fudge in front of Ava Win, whose beloved therapy dog had died right before the school year started. But Robyn hadn't known about the therapy dog. How could she have known?

Yet Alejandra's story. Nestor's story. They hit Robyn

hard. And they made it very difficult for her to keep her anger fueled and hot, which was annoying. Because she wanted to keep her anger fueled and hot. Keeping her anger fueled and hot was the key to not feeling sad about being phase-three-ed. But it was weird. It was like the more chapters of Alejandra, Nestor, and Jonathan got filled out, the more connected she felt to their stories. And the more connected she felt to their stories, the more she knew that she might as well give it up. She would never be able to erase them, let alone hate them. And then what would happen? Then where would she be? She'd be stuck feeling tethered to the very people who had cut her loose. She couldn't let that happen. That would hurt too much.

"Hey," said Lulu. "Speaking of Alejandra, we're so excited to come see your dog-training class." Lulu's mood had changed completely. It was hard to believe she'd been sad only a moment ago.

"Oh," sighed Robyn. "Change of plan." She explained how she'd be training with Mrs. Zazueta now. "We all thought it would be better for Sundae to work with a real, professional agility trainer," she said. "Because he's such a natural at the sport." She spoke matter-of-factly, as if she had been closely involved in the discussion to move Sundae from Nestor's class to his grandma's.

Then, worried that they'd get mad at her all over again, she poured on the regret. "I'm so sorry about that," she explained. "I have to at least talk to the teacher before I can invite anyone. You get it, right? Especially because she's a real stickler. I've seen her in action. But I'm sure you can come sometime soon. I'll make sure. Okay? I promise. Okay?"

"We get it," Marshan reassured her as Lulu looked on, nodding. "But I hope we don't have to wait too long."

"More importantly, what about poor Fudgey?" asked Lulu.

"She'll still be working with Nestor." Robyn said that Nestor and the others wanted Fudge to be their demonstration dog. She followed that with a lie that spilled easily from her lips. "But she's only going to do that because that's what's best for Fudge. Fudge wants to make more dog friends."

"I think Fudgey will like being with the other misfit dogs," said Marshan. "She'll see that there are other dogs like her."

Robyn's head swiveled toward Marshan. "Misfit?"

"Well, she won't *see*, though," said Lulu, who talked over Robyn. "Because her eyes are bad. Remember? But I think you're right. It will be nice for all the misfit dogs to be together."

"Fudge isn't a misfit, though," said Robyn. "Fudge

fits in with everyone. Everyone loves Fudge." She thought about it some more. "Actually, none of the dogs are misfits. They're just dogs. Some of them could do regular agility if they wanted. Well, this one German shepherd could. It belongs to a girl in Nestor and Jonathan's class."

"Which girl?" answered Lulu.

"She wears glasses. She's pretty," said Robyn.

They shook their heads.

"She uses arm braces?" The words had gotten stuck in her mouth, and she colored a bit as she said them. She didn't even know the girl's name, but she was like Fudge, wasn't she? She was more than her disability, right? Her disability wasn't maybe the first words Robyn had to use to describe her.

"Oh, *her*," said Marshan. "That's Emily R." She draped her hand across the bottom part of her mouth. "Yeah, she is pretty. It makes it especially sad that she needs those braces."

"But don't you see," said Lulu like it was the most obvious thing in the world. "*Emily R.* is the misfit in that case. But it's good because that makes it a class for misfit people too."

Robyn froze. She felt like she should explain that this Emily girl wasn't a misfit either. But it was like all her words had vanished, and she didn't know where to find them.

"Whoa," said Marshan firmly. "I don't think you're allowed to call a person a misfit."

"Okay," said Lulu. "But then what would you call the class? Either the people in it or their dogs are very sad cases."

"So maybe it's a sad-cases class," said Marshan.

Lulu nodded. "That's true. Nestor's class is for the sad cases. His grandma's class is for regular people and dogs." She looked over at Robyn. She pouted. "Still, poor little Fudgey."

Robyn's eyes were on her jacket zipper. She still couldn't find her words, but she wanted them to understand that there was nothing sad about anyone in Nestor's class. Some—both people and dogs—had challenges. Some had experienced hard things. But, as far as Robyn could see, they were doing pretty well. She remembered everyone crowding around those little toasts. Talking, laughing, connecting. No glass doors there. No walls or barriers. They were having a great time. They were all doing so well that they didn't even need her. They just needed her dog.

The unfairness of that—how they had the nerve to expect to work with Fudge without her—flared, and then that made all of her anger flare. Her words returned. "You're right. Everyone in Nestor's class is a sad case. Except for Fudge. Fudge is perfect." Instantly, she regretted what she'd said. But she also knew that

that's what happens when you can no longer laugh it off, when you are so close to burning it all down that you can hear the strike of the match.

Marshan patted Robyn's hand. "It's cute you think your dog is perfect. Everyone should think that."

"Yeah," said Lulu. "My cat throws up on my bed all the time, but I still think she's perfect." She smiled at Robyn. "We get you."

Robyn smiled back. She wondered if they did get her. She wondered if she got them. And, just like that, another glass door slid shut, another wall rose from the ground, leaving her, once again, feeling all alone.

CHAPTER 17

TRUE TO HER WORD, Mom had arranged to come and watch Robyn and Sundae's first professional agility lesson. This was about a week after Marshan and Lulu had insisted that Fudge and everyone else in Nestor's class were "sad cases."

Robyn still felt conflicted about that. At the very least, she wanted her friends to realize that perfect dogs weren't measured by how far they could see or what they could hear. They were measured by something else. She just didn't know what it was. And even if she'd known, she would not have wanted to explain it. She wasn't sure where she stood with her rules now. None of the rules seemed to work. Yet all of the rules seemed to think they worked, and they would announce themselves—unbidden. Like royalty, any old time they wanted. And now ever-popular rule number two was waving its crown at her, reminding her that people were judgers. And Lulu and Marshan were perhaps judgier than most. And they some-times seemed pretty close to phase-threeing her themselves, and since Robyn couldn't afford to be ignored and forgotten by every single kid she knew in San Luis Obispo, she let it go.

And, frankly, Robyn figured that she had bigger prob-lems to deal with. Namely, the dropping off and pick-ing up of Fudge from the ability-training class to which Robyn herself was no longer invited. They were all going to be there. Nestor. Alejandra. Jonathan. Every-one else. They were going to be at Nestor's house with their dogs and healthy snacks and one-big-happy-pack-ness. She could imagine them. So joyful. So bonded.

Then she would show up, and it would be a world of awkwardness. Because they would all know that they were trying to erase her, and she would know that she was trying to erase them. But they would stick to their silly game of pretending they were only trying to help Sundae advance, and she would have to stick to her silly game of pretending she believed them. And for those two brief moments of drop-off and pickup, she would also have to pretend that she wasn't trying to erase them at all. She would have to say something to them. And what could she say? It seemed like a hurdle even Gigante couldn't jump.

But Mom to the rescue. As soon as they entered Nestor's backyard, Mom fell into her mom thing, which was also her teaching thing. She surveyed the scene, and she took over.

"Hello. So you're Nestor. And you must be Jonathan. And Alejandra, so nice to finally meet you. I've talked to your dad, of course. Tell me, who else is here? And Nestor, can I meet your grandfather? I want to thank him for keeping an eye on Robyn while she and the dogs have been training here."

A question or two more here. A compliment or ten more there. Boom. Fudge's drop-off was complete. And Robyn hadn't uttered a word.

Sundae began to whine as soon as the gate clicked behind them. He kept glancing back at Nestor's. Twice, he stood stock-still and refused to move forward. Mom had to pick him up and carry him.

"There you go," said Robyn. "He doesn't want to train without Fudge. I told you. We should just take a break from all of this."

"No," said Mom. "Sundae needs to see what we're doing. He'll be okay. This is good for him, Robyn. Give him a chance."

Sure enough, half a block later, Sundae was walking on his own again. But his tail was down. Robyn noticed. And she mentioned it repeatedly. Still, as they got closer, Robyn herself started to perk up. That old dog-training excitement started to stir inside her. And she remembered what Jonathan claimed Mrs.

Zazueta had said: Robyn was a natural. Sundae was a natural. Maybe Sundae could be a champion.

By the time they got to the park, the intermediate agility class members were already lined up, each handler and dog about six feet away from the others. Mom found a bench to sit on, and Robyn ran with Sundae to take her place in the group.

Mrs. Zazueta was talking about the course and the way she had set it up.

Robyn peeked at the other handlers. They were all grown-ups. That was a relief. They'd be easy enough to deal with.

She looked over at the course. It was set up like this: hurdle, hurdle, dog walk, pause table, A-frame. There were also a start box and an end box. Nestor had mentioned these to Robyn. He just didn't see the point of them if they weren't focused on competing, so he'd never incorporated them into what they were doing. Still, Robyn knew what they were. They were taped squares on the ground. One was where the dogs and handlers stood before beginning the course. One was where they finished.

Sundae let out a soft whine.

Robyn pulled out her snacks (low-sodium chicken hot dogs because there was no way she was going to ask Nestor for any of those stinky fish treats). She handed a piece to Sundae.

He took a brief sniff and looked away. His nose started wiggling, and suddenly his eyes were focused on Mrs. Zazueta. His tail coiled tightly. He let out a little yip. Then another.

Mrs. Zazueta stopped talking. "I thought this might happen," she said. She walked over and handed Robyn a little baggie of her famous stinky treats. "Once dogs get a whiff of these, there's no going back." Then she introduced Robyn and Sundae to the class, saying proudly, "My grandson has been teaching these two. He's a very talented trainer himself."

Robyn took a stinky treat and handed it to Sundae. A light seemed to go on in his head, and Robyn could see: *Now*, he was ready. *Now*, he was interested in what was going on.

Mrs. Zazueta told everyone to think about the mini-course she'd set up. "Run it in your mind before you run it with your dog. Where will you position yourself? Where will you move? There's no way you can keep up with your dog. Don't try. Choose your pivot points now so you can navigate between the obstacles as quickly as possible."

Any resistance that Robyn had had to the class fell away. She forgot about Nestor. She forgot about Alejandra. She even forgot about Fudge. She was doing exactly what Mrs. Zazueta asked her. She was imagining herself directing Sundae through the course.

She was seeing it all, where she'd run, where she'd stop and give Sundae each command. And all her love-at-first-sight thrills coursed back inside her as she realized with a start that she'd learned her first intermediate agility lesson. The handler doesn't just run and command. The handler makes a plan.

One by one, the dogs in the class took their turns on the course. Robyn watched them carefully and with growing interest. She could see that most of them weren't as fast as Sundae, but many of them had what Sundae lacked: excellent technical skills. They hit all the contact zones. They kept their butts on the pause table without even being asked. But there were also dogs with weak technical skills. They jumped the hurdle from the wrong side; they missed the contact zones or the end box. There was a real mix of what was meant by "intermediate," and Robyn wasn't sure where Sundae would fit in.

Mrs. Zazueta might have wondered about that too, because when she called Robyn and Sundae up for their turn, her eyes were alight with curiosity and maybe something else. Whatever it was, it reminded Robyn of the look Dad made when he had a good hand at cards.

Suddenly nervous, Robyn pointed at the A-frame. "We barely practiced that one. I'm not sure Sundae will remember."

Mrs. Zazueta cocked her head. Coolly, she said, "Just give it a try."

Mom was giving her two big thumbs-up.

"And . . . I'm not sure about the exit box. We didn't do that with Nestor."

Mrs. Zazueta's lips curled downward. "Just . . . try."

The handler next to her, whose Australian shepherd had whipped through the course better than any other dog there, whispered, "Her bark is worse than her bite."

Robyn looked at him, surprised, and he winked.

It gave Robyn the courage to smile back and then lead Sundae to the starting box. When she got there, she unleashed him and said, "Sit."

Positioning herself between the first and second hurdle, she pointed at the obstacle and hollered, "Hurdle!"

Sundae raced over the hurdle, then, at Robyn's command, the second one.

She ran beside him and pointed at the dog walk. "Dog walk."

At the sound of those words, he veered toward it, then went up the ramp, across the plank, and down the opposite ramp, landing all four paws in the contact zone.

Robyn was waiting near the bottom. He followed her to the pause table and jumped to the top. But he was too eager and immediately moved to jump back down.

"Sit!" said Robyn.

Sundae sat and watched Robyn alertly until she gave the signal for him to get down.

He jumped to the ground.

She pointed to the A-frame. "A-frame."

He zoomed past her. He passed the A-frame and began to run a loop across the course, as if he were thinking, *A-frame? Which one of these is the A-frame?*

She shook her head and ran to the end box. "Sundae. Come here, Sundae."

He ran to her and pounded his front legs into her thighs. He wore his most insistent snack face as he made it very clear that she needed to give him his stinky treat immediately.

She bent down and gave him his treat. "Good job, Sundae."

When she stood up, she realized that the other handlers were all looking at Sundae with open mouths.

"What?" she said, feeling her face grow hot. Was it because he didn't know the A-frame?

She looked over at her mother. Mom had moved closer. Her palms cradled the sides of her face, and she wore a stunned look on her face.

Robyn pointed at Mrs. Zazueta. "I told you he doesn't really know the A-frame."

Mrs. Zazueta cleared her throat. "That was . . . pretty good." Then, without another word or glance at Robyn, she walked to another part of the course and said, "Today, we'll be perfecting our weave poles."

Robyn returned to the group of handlers and dogs.

The Australian shepherd's handler, a young man wearing a sweatshirt with the university's logo on it, whispered, "That was something else."

Robyn swallowed. "Sundae will get better at the A-frame."

"No," he whispered. "Your dog is good . . . and fast. Your dog is super fast."

Robyn felt herself grow a little taller. She said to Sundae, "Did you hear that? You are super fast."

She looked back at Mom. Mom had pulled herself together and was now giving her the thumbs-up sign again. She mouthed, "That was incredible!"

When class was over, Mrs. Zazueta told Robyn to hold back.

Nestor's grandfather had arrived and was now breaking down the equipment and carrying it back to his van. A few of the other handlers were helping.

Mrs. Zazueta waved a hand at Mom, inviting her to come over.

When Mom reached them, Mrs. Zazueta looked at her and said, "You can see that my grandson is an excellent trainer."

"Indeed," said Mom in her most agreeable voice.

Mrs. Zazueta sighed, her grandma pride puffing up her chest. "You know why Nestor's so special? He sees potential. Like your dogs. He saw the potential in them. Even I didn't see it. I'm sorry to say it, but it's true. But Nestor . . . Nestor *sees*."

"Ah!" said Mom, winking at Robyn. "Sounds like he has a growth mind-set."

Robyn rolled her eyes.

But Mrs. Zazueta had tuned Mom out. She looked at Robyn. "We need to teach Sundae the A-frame."

She suddenly started yelling in Spanish to her husband, who had just broken down the device so it would fit in the van.

He looked at her, threw up his arms, and yelled something back before sticking out his gut and setting it up again.

Mrs. Zazueta led Robyn and Sundae over to the A-frame. Mrs. Zazueta gave Robyn a few tips on how to have Sundae approach it, and then they practiced a few times.

"Keep practicing at home," Mrs. Zazueta said. "At this level, dogs need to be training more than once a week." She looked at Mom. "I'll give you a list of equipment. You can get it online. Used is usually just as good as new and can save you some money."

Mom frowned. "Our yard is very small." When

Mrs. Zazueta just kept looking at her blankly, Mom added, "I'll see what I can do."

The silver-haired woman bent down and let Sundae sniff her hand. In a voice that finally seemed to belong to someone who would plant a giant blow-up teddy bear on her front lawn for Valentine's Day, she scratched the back of Sundae's ear and said, "Nice to meet you, Mr. Sundae. You are going to be my little agility champion, aren't you? Yes, you are. I know you are."

CHAPTER 18

IT WAS HARD NOT to love Mrs. Zazueta's class. It was fun and exciting, and Robyn was a natural. Mrs. Zazueta had said so.

So who could blame Robyn? Within a few weeks she'd developed a bit of a swagger, a bit of arrogance. She wouldn't have said that she was *better* than the people in Nestor's class, the people who chose full-size candy bars over her and who thought she was an insignificant speck, but she would have said that maybe she was more of a winner than they were.

One day she sauntered into Nestor's yard.

No one seemed to notice her as she bent down and scratched Fudge's neck. "You be a good girl," she whispered. "I love you." Then she used a touch command of her own invention. She pressed her palms gently against Fudge's rib cage and kissed her forehead. It meant, "Don't worry. I'll be back."

She stood back up, handed Fudge's leash to Jonathan,

and said loudly, "Hi there. Intermediate agility is so great. It's the best class ever. I'm so glad I'm taking it. Bye. Thank you." Then, without another look, she tossed her hair and sashayed away.

Sort of. Sundae started to whine. Then he dug his feet into the grass, and she had to scoop up his squirming body and carry him out the gate.

But the point she hoped they noticed was this: She was off to bigger and better things. She was leaving them far behind. And one day they'd be sorry.

Half a block later she put Sundae back on the ground, and, without resistance, he walked alongside her. "That's right," she said. "It's not bad that we left all of them. What we're doing is better. It's more fun, and one day you'll be a champion, and that's just what you want, right? That's what anyone would want."

Nivien, who was trying to prepare for a test, had been relistening to a college lecture on her AirPods. But she pulled the little white commas out of her ears and said, "What? You okay?"

Robyn glanced up at her. "I was just talking to Sundae, telling him how he'll be an agility champion one day."

Nivien put away her AirPods and readjusted her head scarf. "Champions," she scoffed. "This country is obsessed with champions."

"What's wrong with that?" asked Robyn, sticking

her chin in the air. "Champions are winners. Every-one wants to be a winner."

Nivien opened her hands. "Why?"

Robyn's shoulders rose up to her ears. "Duh. Because winners are the best."

"Do you know what the world's largest living organism is?" asked Nivien.

"Ha!" said Robyn, immediately getting into the game. "A blue whale."

Nivien shook her head. "No. It's a grove of aspen trees in Utah. It covers over a hundred acres and includes over forty thousand trees, all of them con-nected at the root system. Each tree looks separate, but it's part of this larger whole. It *depends* on the whole. If one tree falls, it's like all the other trees have lost a branch. They are many, but they're one."

Robyn blinked. "People in this town are really into trees."

"I'm just saying," said Nivien. "There are no winner aspens. There are only . . . aspens."

Robyn had no idea what Nivien was talking about, and she was grateful when they reached the park and Nivien said, "Look at Sundae's nose wiggle. He knows he's almost at his class."

"I know," said Robyn. "And look at his tail flap. He's excited."

Robyn pulled out the stinky treats Mom had gone

ahead and purchased from Mrs. Zazueta, and she ran to the field of grass where the class met.

Mrs. Zazueta was already getting started. She had them each run a mini obstacle course, and soon Robyn felt fully in sync with Sundae, directing him from one obstacle to the next, her mind focused entirely on what she was doing. It was energizing and fun, and Sundae moved so fast that the other handlers in the class would sigh "Ohhh," and "Ahhh," whenever he raced by.

After a few more classes, the "Ohhhs" and "Ahhhs" were one of the things Robyn liked most about the class. It was as if Sundae's agility were Robyn's, as if his talent were hers. It made her want to stand taller. It made her want to maybe act a little snottier when she went to drop off and pick up Fudge, a little more I'm-better-than-you.

She didn't even always say hi anymore. Or bye. Or thank you. Or even give Fudge a nice neck scratch before giving her the touch command for "Don't worry. I'll be back." She just acted like she was leaving Fudge with the hired help. And it kind of made Robyn feel good, important. And it also kind of made her feel like a jerk, but only if she thought about it, so she tried not to think about it. She tried to think, instead, of how great Sundae was doing.

Once, after dinner, when she and Mom were looking for something to stream, Robyn said, "You should see Sundae, Mom. He's a real show-off. Every time he enters the end box it's like he's saying, 'In your face! I am the champion! Bow down to me!'"

"I don't think that's what he's saying," Mom answered, laughing. "I'm thinking he's saying, 'Give me one of those gross-smelling treats.'"

Robyn laughed too. Because Mom was so obviously wrong. If anyone knew Sundae, it was Robyn. And Robyn knew he was showing off, which was why maybe it unsettled her a few days later when Nestor said practically the same thing.

She, Sundae, and Nivien had returned to Nestor's to pick up Fudge. As usual, Nivien waited outside the gate. Oftentimes, there was still a crowd of handlers and dogs when she arrived, but this time it was just Nestor and Jonathan. They were sitting at the table doing nothing. She glanced inside Mrs. Zazueta's glass door to see Fudge, looking content as could be, lined up next to the poodles.

Nestor jogged inside and got her. Then he said, "Grandma says Sundae's doing good."

"He's doing *great*," Robyn answered, sounding cocky. "You should see him run. He's so fast. He loves it so much."

"You sure it's not the treats he loves?" asked Nestor. He nodded toward Sundae, who was straining against his leash to get to the container of treats left over from ability class.

Robyn pulled him back slightly. "It's not just the treats," she said coldly.

Nestor shrugged. "I just wondered." He sat back down next to Jonathan. They both looked tired and a little bit dusty.

Jonathan said, "Fudge is doing great too. Wanna see?"

Her teeth were clenched, but now they loosened. She didn't want to spend any more time with Nestor and Jonathan than was necessary, but her love for her dogs overpowered all. "Yeah, I wanna see."

With Nestor holding the lure, and Jonathan spotting her, they led Fudge through the tire swing, the hurdle, the dog walk, the pause table, the A-frame, and the tunnel.

Fudge did not go very fast, especially when they reached obstacles like the tire swing, where she needed to use her limited vision to watch her step, but she held her head high, and she moved with confidence, her tail wagging the entire time. And when she was done, she looked ready to go again. She swallowed her treat and trotted back to the patch of grass where they'd started her off.

Robyn went over to her. She bent down. She put her face close to Fudge's so that Fudge could see her. "Good girl, Fudge. You're so clever. Do you like your ability training? Do you?"

"She loves it," said Nestor.

"Yeah," said Jonathan. "She's such a good Gigante. She's everybody's favorite. Huh, Fudge? Nobody can get enough of you." He turned his head and shouted at Mrs. Zazueta's glass door, "Unlike certain poodles I know."

Well, she had to give them this much. They really did care about Fudge. They cared about her enough to talk *to* her, not *at* her. Not everyone was like that with a deaf dog. Not everyone was like that with a *dog*. Period. Sometimes—in the different places they'd lived—Mom would invite her friends from work over. Sometimes she even invited guys that maybe she was, or wasn't, dating. It was never that clear. But if they treated Sundae or Fudge like furniture—ha! That was the last Robyn would ever see of them. Mom knew. How you treated a dog said something about how you treated people. And Robyn knew it too.

She felt the weight of their eyes on her as she remembered how she'd acted when dropping off Fudge earlier. She hadn't said a word to Fudge. She hadn't given her a neck scratch or a forehead nuzzle. She'd just given her the touch command for goodbye and headed out the gate. Now that she thought about it, she could see what a snotty maneuver it had been.

She tipped forward and gave Fudge a kiss, knowing that Nestor and Jonathan must have thought she was a real jerk, and knowing this too: they were right.

CHAPTER 19

"**REMEMBER THAT THING YOU** said about those trees in Utah who are all one living thing because they share the same roots?" Robyn asked Nivien as they walked home.

Before Nivien could respond, Robyn barreled on, not waiting for an answer. "It's because I've been acting like Sundae was better than Fudge, isn't it? But even if Sundae were the best agility dog in the world, he still wouldn't be better than Fudge. It'd be like saying my left foot was better than my right foot. We're a family, a pack. We share the same roots. If one of us falls, the others lose a branch." She cocked her head, a confused look on her face. "Although, technically, I guess packs don't have roots. But you know what I mean."

"Hmmm," said Nivien. "I'm not sure if I meant just the *tree* of you."

Robyn ignored the pun. She was feeling philosophical and didn't want to lose her train of thought. "I know, Mom too. And Dad. But what I'm saying is that . . . it's like . . . you could have the best heart in the world, and people might even say, 'Oh, your heart is so strong that it's the champion of all hearts.' Maybe, your heart might even win a prize. But if your lungs stopped working, you'd keel over, no matter how strong your heart was. The pack needs everyone, and everyone needs the pack, just like how the trees in Utah need all those roots, and the roots need all those trees."

"*Maybe*," said Nivien, leaning hard into that word, "a pack—or a root system—is bigger than most of us can imagine."

"How much bigger?" asked Robyn.

"Oh," said Nivien, letting out a long breath. "I think a *lot* bigger."

They got home to find half a dozen large packages blocking the door.

Robyn took a sharp breath. "The agility equipment." Robyn had known it was coming. She had heard Mom talking to Dad about it, and she knew they'd agreed to go halfsies on a used agility set that included a tunnel, a tire jump, a dog walk, and a pause table.

Robyn grabbed the toolbox, and she and Nivien put the different pieces together. It took them a while, and at first they tried to screw one of the pause table legs onto the top of the table, rather than the bottom, but when they were done they had one very, very crowded mini obstacle course. It looked like a maze or a Rube Goldberg machine. She half expected Nivien to drop a Ping-Pong ball so that they could watch as it was propelled from one device to the next.

"Well, this won't work," Robyn told Nivien as the dogs watched from the other side of the yard. "There's no room between the obstacles."

They debated what to do, finally deciding to stack all the equipment against the fence along the side of the house so that Robyn and Sundae could practice one obstacle at a time.

"We can focus on technique this way," Robyn explained. "Mrs. Zazueta is always saying that technique is super important."

Fudge and Sundae had found their way to her. She turned to Fudge. "And don't worry, Fudge," she said. "I'm going to practice out here with you too. Because your roots are our roots, and don't let anyone tell you otherwise. Nivien can spot you while I guide you, huh, Nivien?"

"Absolutely," said Nivien. "I would love to help with Fudge's training."

A grin spread across Robyn's face. "You know who else will love it? My friends Marshan and Lulu. They're always saying they want to come to see Sundae and Fudge do their dog training. But when I tell them they can actually *help* with the training, they'll totally flip out."

"I bet," answered Nivien. Then she looked at the obstacles stacked against the fence and crossed her arms. She let out a satisfied sigh and told Robyn that they deserved a snack after all their hard work.

They walked back to the kitchen, and Nivien pulled a croissant out of her computer bag.

"Here," she said. "Try this."

Robyn bit into the golden, buttery pastry. She felt her whole body melt. "This is so good," she said.

"I made them," said Nivien, biting into one of her own.

Who knew? Nivien had gone to culinary school and been a pastry chef for six years before deciding to go back to school to become a pharmacist.

"You must be *so old*," Robyn said. She was used to her babysitters being one or two years out of high school. She looked hard at Nivien. As if for the first time, she noticed the small pores on her face, the mischievous brightness of her green eyes.

Nivien put her hands on her hips. "I'm not that old. I've just had an interesting life."

"Well, I'm glad," said Robyn. "Because otherwise you wouldn't know how to make such good pastries."

"I'll tell you what," said Nivien. "You tell me when your friends are coming to help train Sundae and

Fudge. We'll make a snack for them. Something good. Something with a lot of butter."

Robyn nodded. She could see it now. It was all coming together. It was all making sense. She would lead her own ability class, just for Fudge. Lulu and Marshan would be her assistants. And there would be a better snack than even William could bring. And it would be appreciated. She would be appreciated. And it would be so much fun.

She ran the idea by Marshan and Lulu the next morning as they were settling into their desks.

"When?" asked Marshan.

"As soon as you want," answered Robyn.

"How about tomorrow?" said Lulu.

"Tomorrow is great."

"Oh, it will be so much fun," said Marshan. "And then maybe we can teach our cats too."

Robyn had never heard of cats doing agility (or ability), but hey, she'd seen actor cats on TV. If they could learn things, other cats could too. "We'll figure it out," she said, because suddenly everything seemed possible and good. It was not the way she'd expected to bring her dog-training and her school worlds together, but it was still *a way*, and it seemed, somehow, like a path forward.

But the bottom line was this: there was no time for making butter-filled fancy snacks.

There was only Trader Joe's. Nivien took Robyn there after school. They got a tub of sliced mangoes (Lulu's favorite), another tub of hummus (Marshan's favorite), a bag of fresh pita, and a box of crackers.

When Mom came home, Robyn showed her the spread. "I'm going to put the pita and crackers on the nice platter, and I'm going to put the mangoes and hummus in pretty bowls. I'm going to have it all ready for when they come tomorrow. I might even put a tablecloth out."

"Sounds fancy," said Mom, which made Robyn grin. She knew Lulu and Marshan would like fancy.

And they did.

When they arrived at her house the next afternoon, they took a minute to meet Sundae and Fudge and bask in their excitement, but then they went straight to the kitchen and clapped their hands and squealed when they saw how pretty the table looked. And they clapped their hands and squealed again when they saw what the snack was and learned that it was from Trader Joe's.

"My mom loves Trader Joe's," said Lulu.

"All moms love Trader Joe's," said Marshan.

A bit of cracker fell on the floor and Sundae sucked it up right away.

"Look at little Fudgey," said Marshan. "She likes the cracker."

"Poor, cute little Fudgey," said Lulu.

"Aha!" said Robyn. "That's not Fudge. That's Sundae. See? You can't even tell which dog is which because they're both actually just regular dogs."

Lulu tilted her head to one side. "Well, if they were both regular, we wouldn't have to help you with poor Fudgey. She'd be able to do it herself, like Sundae." She pushed out her lower lip and said in a baby voice, "Poor Fudgey."

Nivien had been standing over by the sink, eating a little mango of her own. Now, she coughed abruptly. Her eyebrows popped up as she gave Robyn a look before excusing herself from the room.

"Ummm," said Robyn. "But . . . Sundae needs help too sometimes. He needs a lot of help from Fudge, actually. And I need help from both of them. We all need each other. Because we are all sort of one, but also sort of not one. Basically, we are a pack . . . of roots." She crinkled her nose, knowing that what she was saying was not coming out right.

Marshan and Lulu crinkled their noses too, confusion making their eyeballs tremble.

"The point is," said Robyn, slicing her hands through the air, "Fudge is just as good as Sundae."

They smiled blandly, and she knew they didn't believe her.

A line of frustration creased her forehead, but she

didn't want to lose sight of what they were doing, of the fun they were supposed to have. "Hey," she said, sounding excited. "If you want, we can do our homework while we eat. And we can even help each other with math—or whatever. It's fun that way."

"Homework?" said Lulu. "I didn't really want to do homework."

"Me neither," said Marshan as she piled more pita bread onto a small plate. "But this is a good snack."

"I love mangoes," said Lulu.

"I know," said Robyn. "That's why I got them."

"And you got the hummus for me, huh?" said Marshan. "You really are so nice, Robyn."

And as if the word itself were magic, a blanket of niceness settled over the three of them, and they ate, and Lulu and Marshan showed off their latest cat scratches, and Robyn knew that it was all going to work out just the way she wanted.

But they had come for a reason, to train the dogs, so eventually they made their way outside. The tire jump was already set up, so they started with that.

Robyn said she would demonstrate with Sundae first. She brought Sundae to the jump and told him to sit. Then she moved to the other side of the obstacle and yelled, "Tire!" He ran and leaped through the tire, landing right at her feet and demanding his treat.

Lulu and Marshan squealed their delight, but when

Robyn lifted the lid off the container of Mrs. Zazueta's treats, they moaned and gagged.

"It's awful," said Marshan, pinching her nose.

Lulu threw her arms in the air and ran straight back into the house. She yelled through the window that she wouldn't come out again until Robyn promised she wouldn't have to smell that "disgusting-gross-whatever-it-is."

Robyn yelled back that they had to use the disgusting-whatever-it-is. Sundae demanded it, and it was the scent they used as a lure for Fudge.

Lulu shook her head. "I can't," she said. "I just can't do it. I'll watch instead."

Marshan frowned but promised she could handle it.

So with Marshan holding a treat at the end of a very long pair of tongs and Robyn moving alongside her, they led Fudge to the tire swing, slowing way down as they got close so that Fudge could see the lowered tire and jump over it.

"Hooray!" cried Robyn when they were done.

Marshan shrugged. Sounding like she was missing something, she said, "I don't really see the big deal. Lulu's right. She's not even doing it herself."

Robyn looked at Marshan. "But . . . she's following the scent. It's amazing."

"She's pretty slow too!" yelled Lulu through the window.

Robyn looked at each of her friends in disbelief. "Okay, let me show you something really hard. We'll do the dog walk."

She moved the tire swing over to the side of the yard and started to assemble the dog walk. She put the ramps in place and asked Marshan to help her attach the twelve-foot-long board.

Marshan grimaced. "It looks dirty," she said, but she came over and helped.

They followed the same strategy as before. Marshan held the lure in front of Fudge as Fudge went up the ramp, crossed the board, and then went down the other ramp.

Robyn, again, acted as spotter.

When they were done, Robyn, her eyes bright, said, "Huh? Amazing."

But Marshan wiggled around. "I still don't get the big deal."

Robyn blinked. She motioned again toward Fudge. "She is following that scent so closely that she's not even getting close to the edges of the board. Could you do that? Only ever seeing a foot in front of you?"

"What Marshan means," yelled Lulu, "is that it's just not as fun to watch as when Sundae does it. Show us Sundae."

Robyn took a deep breath as her shoulders fell forward. "Okay."

So, with Marshan now joining Lulu on the other side of the window, Robyn directed Sundae across the dog walk.

From inside the house came the sounds of excited "Hoorays" as Lulu and Marshan cheered and jumped up and down.

"Do it again," said Lulu.

So Robyn had Sundae perform the obstacle a few more times.

"Let's do something else!" yelled Marshan.

So Robyn brought the dogs inside and put the treat container back in the refrigerator. Lulu said they should look up cat pictures on their phones and show each other.

Nivien had collected Robyn's phone. (The whole house was a no-phone zone when there were guests over.) But she must have felt sorry for Robyn. All of a sudden, she thrust Robyn's phone into her hands, and the three girls retreated to Robyn's room.

They sat on the floor, each of them scrolling through pictures.

"I don't know if I could do what you're doing," said Lulu. "I would just want to train Sundae. He looks so good when he's doing agility. I don't mean to sound mean, but watching Fudge is kind of sad."

"Yeah," said Marshan. "You're a good person, Robyn."

Robyn looked up from her phone. "I'm not a good person just because I want my dogs to have the same things."

Both dogs were lying on her bed. Robyn got up and sat next to them. She began rubbing her hand across Fudge's side.

"See? You saying that you just want your dogs to have the same things? That just proves you're a good person," said Lulu.

Lulu and Marshan scrolled through more cat photos.

Marshan got up to stretch. She wandered around Robyn's room, looking at this and that. "I like your elephant lamp," she said.

"I've had it since I was a baby," said Robyn.

"It's cute." Marshan wandered some more. She stopped in front of Robyn's bulletin board. "What's this?"

Robyn saw instantly what she was looking at. Her list of new-kid rules.

Robyn scrambled up, but so did Lulu. And Lulu was closer to the board.

Lulu read, "Rules for New Kids." Her eyes followed the words, and she said, "Did you make this?"

Robyn pulled the list from the bulletin board and threw it in a drawer. "Oh, that's nothing. That's just . . . a thing . . ."

Marshan moved to open the drawer, and Robyn stopped her.

Marshan said, "What's wrong? Why don't you want us to see it?"

Robyn laughed, but she could tell that laughing it off was not going to help her this time.

"I get it," sighed Lulu. "It's because it's so sad that you had to make a list like that. I didn't know it was so sad to move somewhere new."

"Oh, no," said Marshan, resting her hand on Robyn's. "Are you sad now?"

"No," said Robyn, shaking her head. "I'm not sad."

"Is it because you feel like an outsider? I would never want to feel like an outsider." Lulu started to make a tutting sound as she shook her own head.

Marshan started tutting too. "Oh, poor you. But we're your friends now. You don't have to be sad anymore."

"I'm not sad," said Robyn.

"That's right," said Lulu. "Stay positive. You've got us!"

Slowly, Robyn raised her two thumbs-up to the side of her face, and her friends' faces glowed warmly, even as she imagined her own skin growing a little green. Why was it? Why did their words of comfort seem so empty? Why did they make her feel like they weren't her friends at all, like she was all alone?

CHAPTER 20

SOON AFTER LULU AND Marshan were picked up, Nivien came into Robyn's room.

Robyn was lying on her bed, Sundae and Fudge curled up next to her.

"Well," said Nivien. "That was a total nightmare."

Robyn pulled her pillow over her head. "How much did you hear?"

"Oh, I heard everything." Nivien pulled out Robyn's desk chair and sat down. "Can I give you some advice?"

Robyn took the pillow off her head. She pulled herself up onto her elbows.

Nivien took a long, polished fingernail and pushed a strand of dark hair back inside her head scarf. She said, "Some people puff themselves up by acting sympathetic, but really . . . it's almost like they're tourists. It's like they want to see a person's pain, like you might want to see a lion on a safari. They think that if they *see* the pain and feel sorry for the person with the pain, then that makes them good people."

"Doesn't it?" asked Robyn. "It's better than people who think you're an insignificant speck."

Nivien swiveled back and forth in Robyn's chair. "Honestly? I don't know which is worse. Sympathy is very . . . distancing. It keeps you at an arm's length from the person, or dog, you feel sorry for. It *feels* like it's an action—like you've done something—but you haven't really done anything. All you've done is convinced yourself that feeling bad for someone else's suffering is enough. That because you acknowledged it, you don't have to do anything to help."

"Do you think that's how Lulu and Marshan think?" Robyn knew the answer even as she was asking it.

Nivien rested her fist under her chin and looked up at the sea-green paint on Robyn's ceiling. "It kind of seemed like it."

Robyn sat up and scooted backward to rest her back against the wall. "I feel like all they see is the chapter of Fudge that is blind and deaf. And now . . ."

Nivien lowered her gaze to meet Robyn's, but as soon as their eyes locked, Robyn looked away and stared at her elephant lamp.

Nivien said, "You worry that they'll only see the chapter of you that wrote that list?"

Robyn nodded.

"I've wondered about that list," said Nivien.

When Robyn didn't say anything, the babysitter added, "I was always the new kid too. It was hard. But I was also an immigrant, and my English was very limited for a while." She motioned dramatically to her head scarf. It was orange with gold strands, and it made her green eyes even brighter. "And I wear this. People could—can—be mean, even teachers."

She stood up, stretched her back, and started to pace the short distance of Robyn's room. "I never wrote a list like that, but those ideas—all of them— were in my head. I still hear them telling me what to do." She sighed again and plopped back into the chair.

Robyn had met a few new kids in her day, kids who were starting over in a new school or state. But they weren't new kids like her. They hadn't been the new kid over and over and over again. Robyn had always felt a little sorry for them. She was the expert. They were the deer in the headlights. They didn't get that you needed to watch everything, all the time. They didn't understand that you needed to think about cause and effect. That you had to go slow. That you had to make yourself a set of rules, like she'd done. Like, it turned out, Nivien had done.

Robyn rubbed the back of her neck and sighed, grateful to know that Nivien understood, that Nivien had figured it out the same as her. But she also heard, in what Nivien was saying, the challenge of it all, the way the rules—so smart—could try to take over.

Robyn turned sideways so that her legs fell over the bed. "Sometimes I don't even want the rules to be there, but they're still there." She thought of all the times she'd wanted to play handball with Alejandra, Nestor, and Jonathan, all the times she'd wanted to tell Harrison to stick his judgey looks and comments in his ear. But she'd never done it. Not once. She said, "It's like the rules have become the bus driver, and I'm the bus."

Nivien came and sat next to her. "Just try to remember: No matter how it feels sometimes, *you* drive the bus. Not the rules." She let out a deep breath. "But I get it. My rules always try to drive the bus too. One of my old rules was 'Say yes.' Just say yes. Whatever it is. Your mom, she's nice. But I used to babysit for this other professor. She was always making me pick up her dry cleaning or go buy her groceries. I was always thinking, *Say no! I'm not your errand person. I'm your babysitter.* But every time she asked, I would answer, 'Of course. It's my pleasure.' I couldn't stop myself. It's good to help people, but if you never say no, never speak up, you'll be living your life only for others. And that's not how it should be."

"Oh, God," said Robyn. "I'm glad I never thought of the 'say yes' rule." But as soon as she spoke, she wondered if she hadn't been living that rule anyway. How many times had she walked the blacktop with Marshan and Lulu just to please them, just to thank them for being nice to her? As if that were what friendship was. Doing what other people wanted so that they would continue including her in their group.

She looked at Nivien. "So, what's your advice?"

Nivien bent her head forward and thought for a minute. "I guess I don't have any advice after all. But know this: I see your pain. I'm trying not to hold it at a distance. It must be hard, and, in my mind, I'm giving you a big hug."

Robyn threw her arms around Nivien, who hugged her back. And it was weird. Robyn felt not just that her pain had been seen, but that all of her had been. And it felt sad, and mournful, and good.

CHAPTER 21

THE NEXT DAY, MRS. Wang made an unusual addition to the morning announcements. She said the school was starting a new tutoring program. It would be held at lunchtime in the media center. It was purely optional. No one had to go, but it would be a good chance for people to get a head start on homework, and the tutors—all family and community members—were looking forward to meeting them.

At first, Robyn thought, *There is no way I am going to spend my lunch recess working with a tutor.*

But around midmorning, Mrs. Wang called Robyn up to her desk and whispered that she'd love Robyn to give the new program a try. Ever since the tutoring sessions with Alejandra had stopped, math had become even more mysterious for Robyn, and it was showing in her grades.

Robyn, her face turning pink, nodded and returned to her seat.

"We heard," said Lulu, leaning forward. "We're so sorry."

Robyn's face turned even pinker, and she nodded again. She remembered the things Nivien had said, and she whispered, "Maybe it'll be a good thing."

She went to the media center as soon as she finished her lunch, and while it had none of the excitement of handball or, really, anything fun, there was something comfortably familiar about the tutoring program. It was like an activity line. It was a place to blend in and look like you had a purpose. It was a safe escape from the boredom of walking the blacktop again.

It also gave her time to think, and that was good. Nivien had convinced her of something. She could be a perfectly good desk mate to Lulu and Marshan, and she could happily eat lunch with them if they ended up at the same lunch table, but she didn't want to hang out with them anymore. They were not bad people. She knew that. But she wasn't convinced that they were entirely good people either. They only saw people as their saddest chapters. It was wrong and, not just that, it was kind of weird. And Robyn didn't want to hear it anymore, and she also didn't want to be their latest sad case, which she guessed was a little beyond her control. They were judgers. They would judge her, and they would be sad-case tourists wherever they could be sad-case tourists. There wasn't much Robyn could do about that, but she could choose not to participate in their safari of suffering.

Nivien had made her think about something else too. Could there be an opposite of a sadness tourist? Could there be, maybe, a sadness staycationer? A person who only wanted to see their own sadness, but no one else's? She wondered if maybe she'd been that person. All that avoiding judgment, all that fighting fire with fire, all that holding back. It had not just kept people from getting close to her, but it had also kept her from getting close to them.

How else to explain this: How had she only just learned that Nivien used to be a pastry chef? How had she only just learned that Nivien was an immigrant? And how did she still not know what country Nivien was originally from? It was just like with Nestor. It was just like with Alejandra. And honestly, it was even that way with Lulu and Marshan. She'd been so busy thinking about the impression she might make on people—the chapter that they would define her as—that she'd never really wondered about the chapters that filled out the books of everyone else.

It all boiled down to this: Everyone was a big, fat book.

That being the case, it was time to stop being angry at Alejandra, Nestor, and Jonathan. They were like her. They had sad stories, but they weren't only sad stories.

And if she wasn't going to be a sadness tourist or a sadness staycationer, then she was going to have to see the whole books of them. And if she was going to see the whole books of them, then she would have to admit this: They weren't bad people. In fact, they were good people. And if she had to admit that, then she had to admit what she had known deep down inside all along: They hadn't rejected her. Their commitment to Fudge showed that. But, once, there had been an opportunity for friendship with them. She didn't take it. She *chose* not to take it. They watched her make that choice. And so they made choices of their own. And now that door was shut. That wall was built. That chapter was over. It was just too late.

So she found herself escaping day after day to the orderly and unpressured environment of the tutoring program, and when Lulu and Marshan asked her why she didn't walk around the playground with them anymore, she had an easy and true answer. She needed help with her math, and she was getting what she needed.

Of course, Alejandra, Nestor, and Jonathan never went to the tutoring program. Robyn knew they wouldn't. They had their schoolwork under control. But Emily—the girl with the arm braces and the German shepherd—came sometimes. She seldom needed help with math. For her, the struggle was reading, and the tutors would sometimes ask Emily and Robyn to help each other.

The first time the tutors paired them together, Robyn felt the urge to crawl under the table. She had never said a word to Emily, even though she'd seen her in Nestor's backyard many times. She just knew that Emily must think she was a snotty brat.

But if that was what Emily thought, she never let on. Leaning on her arm braces, she came over to Robyn's table, straightened her glasses, and said, "How are Fudge and Sundae?"

"Great," said Robyn, swallowing the word, hoping she wasn't turning red. She didn't even know Emily's dog's name. "How's . . ."

"Max? Max is awesome. Grandma Z. says he might be ready for intermediate agility soon. But I don't know. I think I like Nestor's class."

"Yeah," said Robyn shyly.

The tutoring period ended, and Emily made her way back to the playground, but there was still a little recess, so Robyn wandered the stacks, taking a close look at the books. In the reference area, she found a giant dog encyclopedia. She pulled it out, found a place to sit, and flipped to the first chapter: "Development of the Dog." She read the first paragraph, the words instantly slipping away as she thought about Emily. What would have happened if Robyn had stayed in Nestor's class? Would she and Emily have become friends? Would they have gone to tutoring together? Would they have laughed about what a goof Jonathan was? Or talked about how Nestor wanted to win a Nobel Prize?

When she got home, she asked Nivien if she had ever really blown it when trying to blend in at a new school.

"Ha," laughed Nivien. "Only a million times."

"And then what did you do?"

Nivien thought about it. They were making delicate little sandwich cookies called French macarons. The cookies were airy and the filling sweet and creamy. Every part of them was pink. The recipe seemed like the most complicated thing in the world, but the batter was yummy.

"I did what I always did," Nivien said finally. "I entertained myself."

Yes. Exactly. That was the right answer. That was the answer Robyn had always leaned into too. Entertain yourself and go back to the drawing board. Be patient. Wait. Let friendship come to you. And in the meantime, do your own thing.

She gave Nivien a knowing nod, and she dropped a tiny bit of batter on the floor for Sundae.

About a week later, Emily returned to the media center at lunch. The tutors paired them together again, and they worked until the tutors left, but this time Emily stayed put. She said she wanted to finish her homework. She had a playdate that afternoon and didn't want to study after that.

Robyn wondered if the playdate was with anyone from ability training, but she didn't think it would be right to ask. So she sat with Emily and helped her figure out her reading comprehension questions.

They left the media center, and Robyn said, "That was kind of fun." And—boop—there it was, rule number two, driving the bus: People are judgers. Don't make it easy for them to judge you. "I mean . . . that wasn't so bad . . . for schoolwork. I'm not like a big nerd who only loves school or anything."

But then she remembered what Nivien had told her: "You drive the bus, not the rules."

She took a breath and added, "I kind of am a nerd. Sometimes. I don't even mind homework. I just don't always like it when it's hard."

"Me neither," admitted Emily. "And I like school too."

They walked together until they reached Robyn's classroom, where they said their goodbyes.

Robyn sat at her desk. She was feeling a little like a sparkler, like a match had ignited her and that she was, even at that moment, giving off bright flashes of color. Because here is what she'd discovered: even when the rules tried to boss her, she could boss them right back.

Lulu reached across the table and tapped her hand. "Hey," she said. "We saw you talking to Emily R."

"Why does she need those arm braces anyway?" asked Marshan, a pained look on her face. "It's so sad."

This time Robyn didn't hesitate. Firmly, she said, "Emily is more than a girl with arm braces. She's a whole book of a person. You need to read past that one chapter. And she's not sad. She's cool."

Lulu's and Marshan's mouths were open, and they were looking at Robyn with great concern.

Softly, Robyn added, "You're cool too. But sometimes you're a little blind."

Lulu pursed her mouth. "Oh, how is poor Fudgey, anyway?"

Robyn rolled her eyes. "Ugh," she said. "That's you being blind. Again."

For the next few days, when Robyn walked into the tutoring program, she found Emily sitting with—of all people—Harrison.

When Robyn saw him the first time, he looked at her and said, "What are you looking at, doofus?"

Emily whacked him gently with one of her braces. "Be good. You know you need to be here."

He looked like he might snarl. In a huff, he turned to face the other way.

Emily called over to one of the tutors. "This is Harrison," she said. "He needs help with fractions and decimals even though he will not admit it."

The tutor said she'd be right there.

Emily looked at Harrison. "Stay." Then she joined a different table that was working on reading homework.

Harrison let out a grumpy sigh and flopped back in his seat.

Robyn had no choice. Harrison was sitting at the math tutor's table, and she needed help with math too. She took an empty seat and looked down at her lap.

They both sat in silence until, without an ounce of attitude or embarrassment, Harrison turned to her and said, "She's actually right. I do need help. I just hate fractions and decimals."

Without looking at him, she said, "I need help too. But this has been good."

The tutor glanced over at them again. "Give me one more minute."

They waited a moment more.

Then Harrison said, "The poodles keep getting out at ability. I'm starting to think Jonathan may be right about Bruce."

Robyn turned to him. She hesitated and then asked, "Do they steal the snacks?"

His eyebrows rose in surprise. "No. They want to visit Fudge."

It was her turn to look surprised.

He said, "They're obsessed with her. She's their alpha. If she even swats her tail the wrong way, they back off."

He chewed his pencil for a moment and added, "I think Bruce might be in love with her." He nodded. "Fudge is awesome."

That was all it took. That was the stamp of approval she needed. Anyone who recognized Fudge's awesomeness couldn't be one hundred percent bad, which meant that maybe Jonathan and Alejandra were right. Maybe Harrison wasn't a total jerk.

All of a sudden he burped loudly, and when another kid looked at him, he glowered and said, "Don't look at me. That was Robyn Goblin."

She shook her head and frowned, but game recognized game. It was kind of funny.

Slowly, the kids in the media center—including Harrison and Emily—finished their homework and went outside to play for the last few minutes of recess.

Robyn kept working, and when she was done, she went and retrieved the dog encyclopedia. She was now on the chapter about dog breeds.

The tutor she'd been working with shot her a kind glance. He was the father of a second grader, and he always wore a running suit when he came to school. Robyn wondered if that was his job: running. He said, "Robyn, I'm sure your classmates would love to play with you. You finished your homework. Why don't you go outside?"

She smiled. She'd met lots of grown-ups like the tutor before. They could be found in every school. They'd see a kid sitting alone and think, *Oh, they must be lonely.*

Really, she wasn't. She was disappointed that she'd blown things so badly with Alejandra, Nestor, and Jonathan. She was sorry things hadn't worked out better with Lulu and Marshan. But, just like Nivien, she knew how to entertain herself and wait. And right now, the easiest place to entertain herself and wait was the media center.

"I'm good," she said to the tutor, and she returned to her book.

She was learning a lot of helpful things in those books, and they were paying off in Mrs. Zazueta's class. She'd begun to understand something. Dog training wasn't a way to impose a person's will upon a dog. It was about learning to communicate with another species and learning to listen as that species communicated with you. She had always thought, for example, that a raised scruff on a dog's back was a sign of aggression. In fact, the book said it was a sign of alertness, but alertness could turn to aggression if a dog felt threatened, so it was important to watch a dog's body language.

She saw that firsthand when a new dog started intermediate agility. It was a Pomeranian. It was Sundae's size, but it had long black fur everywhere except its chest, where the fur was shorter and white.

"He looks like he's wearing a little tuxedo," Robyn said.

"Don't be fooled," Mrs. Zazueta told the class. "He may be cute, but Pomeranians are agility beasts. In their size category, they win all the time."

Robyn hadn't realized that there *were* size categories in agility. But it made total sense. Those long legs on the large dogs covered a lot of territory fast. It wouldn't be fair for the little guys to compete against them. Then again, small dogs had advantages of their own. Dogs like Sundae and the Pomeranian had low centers of gravity. That helped them when changing directions and climbing the dog walk and A-frame.

Mrs. Zazueta told the Pomeranian's owner to stand near Sundae. She wanted the man to see Sundae's form as Robyn guided him across the course.

The owner jogged over, but he was moving too quickly for the Pomeranian's liking. The black fur at the base of the dog's neck stiffened. And then, as they got closer to Sundae, it stayed that way.

"Um," shouted Robyn, "Mrs. Zazueta!" She pulled Sundae close just as the Pomeranian lunged forward.

Sundae had moved away just in time, but now he huddled behind her and trembled.

"I'm so sorry," said the Pomeranian's owner, even as the black dog continued to bark and pull on his leash.

"Pay attention, class," said Mrs. Zazueta, drawing the other class members' attention to the spectacle. "That's why you have to be careful. Even well-trained dogs can be unpredictable."

That's why you have to read the dog, thought Robyn. *Even poorly trained dogs signal what they're feeling.*

She looked down at Sundae. He'd moved next to her but was still shivering, his tail down, his jaw loosening and tightening as he yawned and yawned.

She watched him more closely. Yawning was something else she had read about. Yawning could mean a lot of things for dogs. It could mean they were tired. But it could also mean they were stressed out, especially if they kept yawning, and Sundae was yawning as if he hadn't slept in days.

She gave him a treat and walked to the other side of the obstacle course. "It's okay," she told him. "That Pomeranian was just freaking out. He can't hurt you."

Sundae settled down, and that was that, but at the

next class, it was the same thing. He kept yawning again and again.

She felt sure it was because of the Pomeranian. Every time that Pomeranian saw Sundae, he growled and showed his teeth.

"Mrs. Zazueta," she said after class. "That Pomeranian is stressing Sundae out. I'm not sure what to do."

Mrs. Zazueta listened as her husband began to dismantle the course. She yelled something to him in Spanish, and when he threw his arms in the air and mumbled at her, she crossed her arms and cleared her throat.

Then she turned to Robyn. "Yes. I've noticed. You just have to keep coming back. He'll get over it. This happens sometimes, even at the competition level. He's got to get used to it. It's actually a good thing. It'll give him practice."

Robyn frowned. What she really wanted was for Mrs. Zazueta to kick the Pomeranian out of class for bad behavior, but that clearly wasn't going to happen. So she just put down her head, did her work, and then, later, asked Mom what she thought.

They were having dinner, spicy Indian pancakes made with potatoes and spinach, one of Robyn's favorites.

"I think we learn by persevering," Mom said. "So I guess I agree with Mrs. Zazueta, just keep trying."

"I think maybe Sundae's remembering those coyotes. Like, maybe he's even having flashbacks from his Arizona days. Is that possible?"

Mom got a curious look on her face. "Interesting." She pulled out her phone.

"No phones at the table," said Robyn, her voice surly.

"This is different," Mom said. "It's educational." She typed something in her phone and then bit down slightly on her lip as she read. "Well," she said at last. "You might be right. Dogs who've experienced trauma can have flashbacks. That other dog might be triggering them."

"So what can we do?" asked Robyn, looking over at Sundae, who was fine now. He was happily sniffing at the trash, as if nothing bad had ever happened.

Mom held her fist under her chin and seemed to think about it. "The website I'm looking at says you have to slowly desensitize them."

"What does that mean?"

"It means you have to slowly get them used to the thing that's scary," said Mom. "You should tell Mrs. Zazueta more about Sundae's past. See what she thinks."

But Robyn didn't want to tell Mrs. Zazueta more about Sundae's past. If she told Mrs. Zazueta about the hoarder, and the seventy neglected dogs, and the coyotes picking the dogs off, she worried that Mrs. Zazueta would have one of two reactions. She'd either say, "See! That's why I never thought he should do agility in the first place. He's too traumatized," or, "See! That's why Sundae needs to train with the Pomeranian, so that he can be desensitized." Either way, Sundae would lose. In the first case, he (they) might have to stop agility altogether. In the second case, he might have to suffer more than he could bear to suffer.

The person she wanted to talk to was Nestor. Mrs. Zazueta might have been the experienced dog trainer, but Nestor *got* dogs. He really seemed to know what was going on in their heads. She felt for sure he'd have some ideas on how to help Sundae, but reaching out to Nestor didn't seem like a choice, not after everything. So she returned to agility determined to simply keep Sundae out of the Pomeranian's way. It worked pretty well. If she stood to one side or sometimes moved behind a tree, the Pomeranian wouldn't notice Sundae, and Sundae wouldn't notice it. Until, that was, it was time for Sundae to do any of the obstacles.

Then the Pomeranian noticed. And it barked. And it spat. And Sundae would yawn and shiver and shiver and yawn.

"Trust the process," Mrs. Zazueta urged Robyn.

But Robyn did not trust the process. All she saw was that Sundae, once so good at agility, was now a total mess.

Mrs. Zazueta clapped her hands. "Okay, come closer."

Robyn stood behind the tunnel, blocking Sundae from view, as Mrs. Zazueta explained that they were going to learn the final and most challenging agility-training obstacle: the seesaw.

The seesaw was exactly that, a kid's teeter-totter. To master the seesaw, a dog needed not just precision, balance, and speed, but it also needed nerves of steel. The dog had to walk up the lowered end of the board and keep walking even as its weight caused the board to drop from one side to another. And, for some dogs, that moving board was simply too unpredictable and scary. For that reason, the seesaw often marked the end of a dog's advancement in agility. It could be the fastest, most technically skilled agility-trained dog in the world, but if it couldn't handle the pressure of the seesaw, it would never be a champion.

"But don't worry," said Mrs. Zazueta, looking briefly at Robyn. "We're going to take it slowly."

She asked everyone to gather around the obstacle, but Robyn stood and watched from where she was.

A ramp had been placed under one side of the seesaw, making it level, like a diving board.

Smart, thought Robyn. She could see what it meant.

It meant the dogs could learn the seesaw like it was a dog walk. They would climb the ramp and begin to cross the board. Only when they reached the mid-point would things begin to change. The board would then begin to descend with each new step the dogs took, until, finally, the dogs could step straight from the contact zone right onto the ground.

Mrs. Zazueta told everyone to line up with their dogs. She said, "A lot of dogs, when the board begins to go down, jump straight to the ground. It's okay. If that happens, go with it. Give your dog a treat and just move to the end of the line so they can try again in a little while."

Sure enough, most of the dogs—all but the Australian shepherd—jumped from the board their first few times practicing the obstacle. But quickly, the dogs figured out what was expected of them. They also realized that, with the right balance, one that kept their center of gravity close to the board, they had nothing to worry about. It was just a different kind of dog walk.

But Sundae did not figure it out. Already nervous from the Pomeranian, he jumped every time the board began to drop. And the closer he got to the obstacle, the more he started to yawn.

"It's that Pomeranian," Robyn told Nivien as they walked to pick up Fudge. "That Pomeranian shouldn't get to be there. It's too aggressive."

But the next week, the Pomeranian wasn't there. Its owner had a work conflict and couldn't come. And still Sundae struggled with the seesaw.

The week after that the same thing happened.

By this time, the other dogs in intermediate agility were able to do the device without the ramp.

But not Sundae. Even with the Pomeranian gone, he had come to the opposite conclusion of the other dogs. Instead of deciding the seesaw was just a different kind of dog walk, he'd decided that every dog walk might now be a seesaw. His tail would curl under him as soon as Robyn tried to walk him by a ramp, and he would start yawning all over again.

One week later, the other dogs were flying across the seesaw like they'd been doing it forever. And the Pomeranian was gone for good. Its owner's work had suddenly picked up, which meant they'd had to drop out of the class.

But now Sundae refused to climb any ramp. When directed to do so, he would lean backward or turn in circles, yawning and panting, his eyes wide and full of fear.

Everyone could see he was stressed.

Mrs. Zazueta said, "Don't worry. He's a natural. When he's ready, he'll do it. Just keep trying and follow his lead."

But Mrs. Zazueta's reassurance was wearing thin.

"He's getting *more* stressed, not less," Robyn told the trainer between gritted teeth. "I don't think this is working anymore."

"Sometimes it's two steps forward, one step back. He'll be okay," replied Mrs. Zazueta, who sounded rushed and a little annoyed, as if she'd had enough of Robyn's doubts.

But Robyn's doubts persisted, and she was beginning to think that maybe they needed to drop out of agility themselves. She didn't want to. She would hate it. But if Sundae didn't like it, if it scared him, was it worth doing?

She talked to Mom. She talked to Dad. She talked to Nivien. She consulted the dog encyclopedia, but no one offered any advice that seemed very helpful. It was a choice between "Just keep trying" (Mom, Nivien), "Listen to your gut" (Dad), and "Don't let your dog eat cat poop" (the dog encyclopedia). But these solutions seemed to miss the most important consideration of all: What was best for Sundae? What did Sundae really want?

One day, when she was in the tutoring program, Harrison said loudly enough for everyone to hear, "I don't know why we even have to learn fractions and decimals. I never use them in real life. And when I grow up, I'm going to be a poet, so I'll never have to use them then."

Robyn was seated nearby. Without thinking too much about it, she repeated what Mom always told her when she said things like that: "When you work on hard things, it makes your brain stronger. Even poets need strong brains."

He gave her a skeptical look and snarled, "That sounds like grown-up gobbledygook."

"Maybe," said Robyn. She had gotten better at ignoring his surly side and didn't even look up.

Emily was seated next to Harrison. "You're gobble-dygook, Harrison. Robyn's right. You have to do things that are hard. My mom says so, and she's a teacher so—duh—she would know. She says if you stick with things that are too easy, you're just twiddling your thumbs. But if you try things that are too hard, you're just, 'Ack! This is too hard! I want to cry.'"

"I do not want to cry," snarled Harrison. He threw his pencil across the room, and it landed with a thud against a book. The librarian's head swung toward him, sending her glasses sliding down her nose. She readjusted her glasses as Harrison pointed at Emily.

The librarian's eyes lingered on the pair of them for a moment longer, then she turned in her swivel chair and looked down at her computer.

"The point is," said Emily, "that it's like Goldilocks. Things have gotta be just the right amount of hard."

Robyn was leaning forward in her chair, her hands

on her knees. She wondered what "just the right amount of hard" might mean for Sundae. She wanted to ask what they thought, but she liked the little bit of easiness she'd developed with Emily and Harrison. She didn't want them to think she was being a prima donna again and just navel-gazing about what might seem to them awfully good problems to have. Like: "Oh, my special advanced dog. He can do so much more than *your* dogs, but he's got it so hard."

Boom! She realized: That was her rules talking. They were trying to drive her bus. *Not this time*, she told herself. She sat taller and looked over at Emily. "Can I ask you a question? How would you figure out the right amount of hard for a dog? Sundae is having a really hard time with a new obstacle. Mrs. Zazueta says we need to keep trying. She says he'll get there eventually. But I'm worried that it scares him so much that he's starting to hate agility."

Harrison leaned forward. "What's the obstacle?"

"The seesaw. He won't even do it for one of Mrs. Zazueta's dog treats, and he's obsessed with those."

Harrison's hands flew up and landed on top of his head. He let out a low whistle. "The seesaw? Jeez, Nestor said even he didn't know how to teach the seesaw."

"Yeah, it looks really hard," said Emily.

Robyn sat back. "I think maybe I shouldn't make

Sundae learn it, but Mrs. Zazueta won't listen to me."

Harrison got up and said, "I'll be right back."

But he didn't come right back. And soon the tutors packed up and left.

There were still ten minutes of recess left, so Robyn put away her math and retrieved the dog encyclopedia. She showed it to Emily, who moved closer so that she could see it too. They had just read how the part of a dog's brain devoted to smell is forty times bigger than in human brains when a voice said, "We know what Sundae needs."

It was Alejandra. She was standing right in front of Robyn with Harrison, Jonathan, and Nestor.

Robyn's stomach dropped. She couldn't remember the last time she'd spoken with them at school. And, lately, while she'd been trying to act more appreciative when she dropped off and picked up Fudge, she also knew how snotty she'd been earlier. And she knew that snottiness could be hard to forget or forgive.

"We are ready," said Jonathan, "to offer you an ability-training exclusive: a private class, just you, Sundae, Nestor, Alejandra, and me."

"And Fudge," said Alejandra. "Fudge would want to come."

"Right. You have to bring Fudge," he added. "Now, if you were just some regular dork, we'd make you pay big money for this opportunity."

"No, we wouldn't," said Nestor.

"The point is," said Jonathan, not even letting Nestor finish, "we're giving you the friend discount, which means you're gonna need to bring more of those Rice Krispies treats."

"No, she doesn't," said Alejandra.

"What about me?" asked Harrison. "If Grapey's going, I should get to come. It was my idea."

"And if Harrison is going, I should get to go too," said Emily.

"You can both come, and you can both bring your dogs," said Alejandra. She turned to Harrison. "And don't call me Grapey, you big ol' pile of stinky farts."

"You're a *purple* big ol' pile of stinky farts," said Harrison.

"See? This is why Max and I need to be there," said Emily. "Harrison, I will sic Max on you. Just wait and see."

Alejandra crossed her arms. Her eyes were bright and she was hiding a smile. "Well, the *Guinness Book of World Records* called. They said, 'Congratulations!' You are such a big pile of ol' stinky farts that they want to write a whole page about you in their next book."

"Well, your mother called—"

She cut him right off. "Don't you talk about my mother."

"Enough." Nestor looked at Robyn. "The point is, I think I know how to solve your problem."

Robyn looked at all the faces gathered round her. She had not expected so much kindness, and she didn't really think she deserved it. But she did feel the wall between them descend just a little, and she knew this much: she would take it.

CHAPTER 22

ROBYN, SUNDAE, AND NIVIEN walked from the park to Nestor's house. They had just finished intermediate agility. They were doing more than picking up Fudge. They were taking Sundae to his one-on-one class with Nestor.

"How do you feel?" asked Nivien.

"Pretty nervous," said Robyn. "What if it's a setup? What if, when we get there, they just go, 'Ha, ha. You don't deserve our help.'"

"Come on," chided Nivien. "Do you really believe that will happen?"

Robyn shrugged. "I guess not."

"Me neither. Don't listen to those rules in your head. Don't let them drive the bus. Just get in there and be you."

Be me? thought Robyn. *Which me?*

"I'm just going to go in there," she said, "and I'm going to see how it goes."

"Great idea," said Nivien, briefly resting her hand between Robyn's shoulder blades. "And remember, what's your secret weapon?"

Robyn nodded toward a box that Nivien was holding. "French macarons."

"That's right," said Nivien. "French macarons are the overlooked key to world peace."

Robyn leaned her face toward the box and smelled. These were different macarons from the ones she and Nivien had made before. These were chocolate (dark brown with dark ganache filling) and hazelnut (almond-colored with white buttercream filling).

"Those are the best macaron flavors of all," Nivien had said when they were making them. "Don't believe anyone who tells you otherwise." They were delicious. Robyn was convinced that Nivien was right. They could probably bring peace to the world if people just took a minute to try one.

They got to Nestor's. Nivien handed Robyn the box of cookies, and then Robyn and Sundae walked to the gate.

A moment after she knocked, Nestor let her in and she saw everyone: Jonathan, Alejandra, Emily, Harrison, even William and the two other middle schoolers. And, of course, all the ability-training dogs were there too, all except Fudge. She was inside Nestor's house, dozing next to Bruce.

Robyn unleashed Sundae and he trotted over to the other dogs, ready to give them each a polite butt sniff.

Then she made her way to the group of kids standing in a huddle near the table.

Nestor said, "How did it go in intermediate agility?"

"The same," she said. "But, you can see, he's doing better now."

"Umm-hmmm," muttered Nestor.

She swallowed. "I'm really glad you guys are helping," she told him.

"That's what packs do. They help." His voice was as gruff as ever, and Robyn wondered if he was saying that Sundae was in their pack, or if she was.

They reached the rest of the group and she held out the box.

Jonathan rubbed his hands together. "There better be chocolate in there."

She said, "I made these with my babysitter. She used to be a pastry chef."

"Nivien?" said Alejandra, surprised.

"Yup." Robyn opened the box to reveal the pretty sandwich cookies. She said, "They're French macarons, and they're really good. And since this is an extra class, I thought maybe we didn't have to eat like athletes."

Jonathan grabbed a handful of cookies. "That makes perfect sense."

Robyn put the container on the table and watched it empty out as everyone took a few cookies.

She turned to see Nestor licking his fingers, a tiny bit of buttercream on the corner of his mouth. He dabbed it away with his tongue and then motioned for Robyn to follow him over to the seesaw.

The seesaw stood in the very back of the yard, and judging by the leaves and dust on it, it didn't get much use.

Nestor took a deep breath and let it out. "Okay," he said. "Here's what I think. Alejandra told me a long time ago about what Sundae's and Fudge's lives were like before you adopted them. And Grandma told me about the Pomeranian. I think maybe the Pomeranian reminded him of how scary it was to be hunted down by coyotes."

"That's just what I think!" Robyn said. "And I know we need to get him used to dogs with attitude and stuff, but—I don't mean to be mean—it seems like maybe your grandma is trying to get him used to things too fast."

"Yeah," said Nestor, putting his hands in his jeans pockets. "I don't think so. 'Cause Grandma says the Pomeranian is gone now, and so if it was just the Pomeranian reminding him of the coyotes, he'd be better."

"Okay," said Robyn. "But what if the seesaw and now all the jumps remind him of the Pomeranian?"

"No," Nestor said, leaving no room for disagreement. "You're making things too hard." He stopped for a second, a thoughtful look on his face. Then he pointed at her. "You do that sometimes. You overthink."

She clasped her hands atop her head and sighed, knowing he was right.

"You got two problems," he said. "You've got the aggressive dogs freaking him out problem. That's the one with the Pomeranian. And then you've got the treat problem."

"Treat problem? But he loves your grandma's treats."

He shook his head. "You don't get it. He loves the treats *too* much. He is more motivated by the treats than the sport. Any dog like that? It's gonna catch up to them. Something, like the seesaw, is going to seem scary, and they're going to have a problem."

Robyn dropped her hands. She turned and found Sundae. He was staring longingly at Jonathan, who held a hazelnut macaron in his hand. Nestor had hinted at Sundae's treat obsession before. So had Mom. Robyn hadn't believed either one of them. Sundae had always seemed so happy doing agility—at least until the Pomeranian. It couldn't have all been about the food. Could it?

Nestor seemed to read her mind. "He still likes agility, and it's been good for him. He just needs a better motivator to get him past his fear."

"But what could that be?" asked Alejandra.

Nestor flashed a look at Jonathan, who was now munching on the hazelnut cookie, even as he reached for a chocolate one. He said softly, "When I had . . . cancer . . . the thing that motivated me was my family." He shook his head. "What I'm saying is that I think Sundae needs his whole family to help motivate him. He needs you," he said, looking at Robyn. "But he also needs Fudge."

"Fudge," said Robyn, it all seeming so obvious now. "Of course."

"Fudge is his dog dog whisperer," said Nestor.

All of a sudden, Alejandra was standing next to him. "I get it," she said. "You want Fudge to be Sundae's emotional support dog."

One corner of Nestor's mouth pulled up. "Pretty much. She's always given a lot of emotional support to Sundae, and now he needs Fudge again. He needs her to help him learn the seesaw."

So they got to work.

Nestor hollered to the group to gather round. He told Jonathan and Alejandra to prop up one side of the seesaw with one of the dog-walk ramps.

"Everybody else just do what you were doing," he said. "We don't want Sundae to feel like he's back in class."

Jonathan dropped his side of the ramp, leaving Alejandra's eyes bulging as she tried to hold up the whole thing by herself. He clapped his hands. "Just do what you were doing, people," he said, "Just talk and stuff."

Nestor rolled his eyes and tossed his head as he muttered, "I just said that."

When the ramp was finally set up, Robyn leashed up Sundae, and Nestor brought Fudge back outside, even as the poodles howled their sorrowful goodbyes. Then, with Fudge beside him, and Sundae beside Robyn, they made their way to the seesaw.

Sundae's tail dropped. He started to yawn, and he suddenly let out a high-pitched whine.

Nestor and Robyn stopped.

Over by the table the conversation fell quiet. The other handlers might have been trying to act like nothing was going on, but, clearly, they were paying attention.

"Well," said Nestor, "I'm not so sure now. I don't want to push Sundae too much."

"That's what *I* always say," said Robyn.

Jonathan and Alejandra had been watching from behind the ramp.

"Can we . . . I have an idea," said Alejandra, coming forward.

Robyn and Nestor both nodded.

"Emily, William," she called. They walked over to

her. She handed them each a bag of stinky treats and directed them to the end of the ramp. "And now, Harrison, you stand here with Jonathan. And just follow my lead."

Harrison walked over to Jonathan.

Alejandra grabbed a treat with the trusty barbecue tongs. Then, with Nestor holding Fudge on a very short leash, and Jonathan and Harrison serving as spotters, she used the scent of the treat to guide Fudge up the ramp.

Keeping her own leash short, Robyn had Sundae follow right behind Fudge. His tail was low, but he kept his eyes on Fudge and made his way to the top.

Alejandra guided Fudge to the midway point of the seesaw and gave Fudge a treat.

Behind Nestor, Fudge, and her team of spotters, Robyn gave Sundae a treat.

Then, slowly, slowly, slowly they moved the dogs forward along the descending board until they reached the bottom.

There was a collective exhale as Emily and William plied both dogs with treats.

Then, as one, the group burst into cheers, and Sundae—surprised by the noise—ran under the table.

They tried it again, and again, and again. Quietly. Each time, Sundae's tail rose a little higher, and his eyes looked a little brighter, and when he could follow Fudge across the board with ease, they stopped.

"We don't want to do too much too soon," said Nestor.

Robyn nodded. "I agree."

"Yeah," said Emily, taking a step forward. "The Goldilocks principle. Not too hard. Not too easy. Just right."

"I like that," said Alejandra, impressed.

"I invented it," said Harrison, and Emily thwacked his leg with her arm brace.

Robyn couldn't help herself. She snorted, and with that snort a heavy weight seemed to lift off her. She looked around. Boy, did she like these people, this place, this moment. And, boy, did the fragile quality of it all scare her.

Nestor's backyard grew quiet, and Robyn said softly, "I feel like you guys shouldn't be so nice to me."

Jonathan pointed at her, a knowing look on his face. "Ha! That's because you've been icing us out." His gaze moved from Nestor to Alejandra.

Embarrassment and shame shone red on her cheeks. She remembered those early days after Halloween and how she'd been so cold to them. She twisted her head and looked down at the ground as she said, "I thought . . . you didn't want to be my friends."

Alejandra said softly, "I wanted to be your friend. We thought . . . we weren't your type."

Robyn's shoulders fell forward. Awkwardly, she said, "I don't think I knew what my type was." She began to wring her hands. "I'm sorry. It's hard for me sometimes. I always think . . . people are going to judge me for . . . everything."

Alejandra dropped her chin. Then she ran the back of her sleeve against her nose. Frowning, she said, "I don't know if you knew this, but my mom and brother got deported to Argentina a few years ago."

Harrison stuck out his chin. "Anyone who would make a mom leave a kid is a real butthead. And if you want, I will find out who did it, get their address, and send them a harsh poem. Like, *really* harsh. You don't even know how harsh it will be."

Alejandra's expression relaxed. She said to Harrison, "You're a butthead."

Then she stretched her tongue down to her chin, squeezed tight her eyes, and went, "Aggggh. I hate this."

She opened her eyes and, with a calm look on her face, said, "Before she had to go, my mom took me shopping. She said she was going to get me enough clothes, in enough sizes, so that I'd have enough of everything until she returned. Back then, my favorite color was purple, so I made her buy everything purple." She let out a deep sigh. "It's *a lot* of purple."

She shook her head, and she seemed to collapse

for a moment under all that purple. But then a spark seemed to ignite inside her. She straightened her spine. She said, "But that's what I wanted, and that's what I have, and that's what I'll wear until my mom comes back and buys me new things. I don't care what people think. That's their problem. Not mine." She turned to Robyn. "What other people think is their problem, not yours."

Robyn sighed and looked at Alejandra. She was wearing purple jeans, purple sneakers, and purple socks. The purple bottom of her purple shirt hung below her purple windbreaker. Robyn cocked her head. She didn't know how she'd ever thought this girl was radioactive or not bendy in the windy. If anything, Alejandra was the opposite of those things. She wasn't boxed in by concern about what others might think. She wasn't governed by worry. She was like an aspen or a dog. She was strong, and she made everyone around her feel stronger, just by being herself.

Robyn wondered what that must be like, to drive your own bus all the time, or even most of the time. It would seem like freedom, she thought. It would seem like you could go anywhere, or even stay anywhere. It wouldn't matter. Because no matter what, you wouldn't be alone. You'd have your pack. You'd have your groove. You'd have people.

CHAPTER 23

THE NEXT DAY AT school Marshan and Lulu told Robyn they needed to talk to her.

"We're worried about you," said Lulu. "You always go to the media lab for lunchtime tutoring. It seems like a cry for help."

"And we are ready to help you," said Marshan. "Eat with us at lunch, and you can tell us all about your problem."

Robyn gazed across the room. She caught Alejandra's eye, and Alejandra—dressed in a purple down vest and purple velour pants—gave her a thumbs-up.

"I can't," said Robyn. "I'm playing handball at lunch."

It felt weird running up to play handball after so long, and she wondered if she could even call herself the Queen of Handball anymore. But she knew what her type was now, and her type was the type that forgave you when you acted like a jerk. And her type was the type that played handball and trained dogs. She'd lost sight of her type once; she wasn't doing it again.

Alejandra ran up next to her. "You're playing handball? Yeah! Finally, some competition around here." She paused for a minute and looked both ways. Then she added, "That's not bragging. That's just stating the obvious."

Bing, bang, boom. Nestor beat Jonathan and Emily.

Bing, bang, boom. Nestor beat some kid Robyn didn't know.

Bing, bang, boom. Harrison beat Nestor.

Bing, bang, boom. Alejandra beat Harrison.

Bing, bang, boom. Alejandra beat Robyn.

"Don't feel bad," Alejandra said to her. "You're just out of practice. You're still pretty good."

Robyn felt winded and tired, and the base of her fist was covered in dust. She bent down to catch her breath. When she looked up, she felt like a new kind of blending in had begun. It was a good kind of blending in. It made her feel strong, like Alejandra, and she knew that she would need that strength the next time she went to intermediate agility.

Nivien was by her side as they approached the class.

"You know what you're going to say, right?" asked Nivien.

"Yup," said Robyn.

"And you'll just do it."

"Right."

Mrs. Zazueta was finishing setting up the tunnel. Robyn, with Sundae at her side, ran up to her.

She said, "Mrs. Zazueta, I'm not going anywhere near the seesaw or the dog walk today. It's too scary for Sundae without Fudge. Nestor says—"

Mrs. Zazueta cut her off. "It's fine. I've talked to Nestor." She pushed her lips forward. "You know, he really is pretty amazing. This whole ability thing . . . all the techniques he's invented."

"It is pretty cool," said Robyn. "But . . . I should tell you . . . it's been kind of a team effort. Everyone has had ideas, although, definitely, Nestor . . . is the leader of the pack."

"Huh," said Mrs. Zazueta. She scratched her arm and looked at the other participants, who were beginning to line up for class. "You know," she said casually, "that's a myth. Dogs don't really have pack leaders. They all just do their thing, but together. And they do depend on each other, help each other. They're not meant to be alone."

Maybe none of us are meant to be alone, thought Robyn.

Class began, and Robyn did just what she'd said she would. She worked with Sundae on everything Mrs. Zazueta had laid out, except the obstacles with ramps. Sundae zipped through the tunnel and weave poles. He launched himself over and through the jumps and across the A-frame. He was going at his own speed. And he was finding his confidence again.

When she got to Nestor's, Sundae had more energy than he'd shown in a long time. He zoomed across the lawn, bending his forelegs into a play pose when he saw Fudge across the glass door, sitting with the poodles.

Nestor brought Fudge back outside, her tail wagging. She was ready too. She was ready to dog-whisper her buddy Sundae across that seesaw.

They practiced just like they had the last time. Then they had Fudge, alone, still leashed and with her team, cross the board over to Emily and her bag of treats.

When she was done, they had Sundae, alone, still leashed and with Robyn, cross the board over to William and his bag of treats.

And when that worked, they did it again and again and again, until finally, at the end of the class, they were able to have each dog try to cross the obstacle without a leash.

And, as if he'd been doing it forever, Sundae calmly walked up the ramp, crossed the board to the mid-point, and then walked down the descending board.

"And that's ability training," said Alejandra.

"Trademark Nestor Zazueta," added Jonathan.

A satisfied grin on her face, Robyn said, "It just goes to show that with a little emotional support, you can do a lot."

She told Mrs. Zazueta about Sundae's progress at the start of the next intermediate agility class. "We still have to teach him to do it without the ramp, but he's getting there."

"Nestor told me," Mrs. Zazueta said. "What do you think? Gonna try it with him here?"

Robyn shook her head. "I don't think he's ready to do it without Fudge. I'm going to do just what I did with him last time."

"You know what's best," said Mrs. Zazueta, and that was that. But after class, Mrs. Zazueta asked Robyn to hang back. She said she had something she wanted to talk to her about.

"I'm mentioning this to a few of the people in class. The regional California Canine Club's annual agility competition is coming up. There is a category for dogs who've never competed before. I know Sundae has had some setbacks, but if he can get past them, I think he'd be great. He's looking good out there. He's so fast. I'm not saying he'd win, but I'm not saying he wouldn't win. What do you think?"

Robyn bit down on her lip. She didn't know what she thought. She supposed she should feel happy, excited. Who wouldn't want a champion dog? Who wouldn't want to be a champion handler? So why didn't she feel that way? "When is it?" she asked.

"About a month," said Mrs. Zazueta.

That made it easy. "Oh, I don't think he'll be ready."

"You sure? It seems—"

"Nope. I don't think so," said Robyn, grasping for reasons why. "See . . . it's not just the seesaw. What if there's another Pomeranian situation? I don't think he could handle that. Not in only a month."

Mrs. Zazueta crossed her arms. "I see your point. Being afraid of bossy dogs can be harder to overcome. How about this? You give it a try. You think of it as practice, as a way to get some experience in the competition ring."

"I'll think about it," said Robyn, but a stubborn sense of resistance had settled over her. She didn't want to think about it. She didn't want Sundae to compete, and it completely confused her. When she had started intermediate agility, she had hoped for this very moment, this invitation to take herself and Sundae to an even higher level in the sport. So what was the problem now?

Nivien had overheard Robyn's conversation with Mrs. Zazueta. When they made their way to Nestor's for another one-on-one training session, she said, "You don't seem very happy for a person whose dog has just been singled out to compete in some big event."

"Yeah. No. I know."

"So . . . what's the deal?"

"I'll tell you when I've figured it out myself."

They reached Nestor's. Nivien had been carrying a box of mini lemon cakes, each the size of a small can and with a twist of lemon peel on the top. It was their latest creation. ("The lemon peel is what gives it oomph," Nivien had said.) She handed the box to Robyn, and Robyn walked up to the gate.

Jonathan let her in this time, and when he saw the box, he took it from Robyn and gave it a deep sniff. He said, "Okay. Where are the ones for everyone else?"

Alejandra rolled her eyes. She came and took the box from Jonathan and started passing out the small desserts.

Straightaway Nestor said, "What's wrong?"

Robyn sighed. He was an observant one, that Nestor. She scratched her head and told everyone what Mrs. Zazueta had said about competing.

"So what's the problem?" said Emily. "If he's ready, he'll do great. If he's not, he'll get good practice."

"Yeah, and we could do a lot to get him ready," said Alejandra.

"We could up his practice," said Jonathan. "Make it twice a week. Maybe more near the end. But it's gonna cost you more of these little cakes."

"No, it's not," said Emily and William and the two

other middle schoolers at the exact same time.

From the corner of her eye, Robyn saw a flash of movement. She turned to see the poodles running off with the box of lemon cakes.

Sundae, Strudel, Tiger, Max, and the old pug and pit bull chased after them.

"Bruce!" yelled Jonathan, trailing behind them. "Leave it, Bruce! Leave it!"

There was a collective sigh of resignation. Then Harrison said, "I'm kind of rooting for the poodles."

"So what do you think?" said Nestor.

She bit her thumbnail. "I don't know. I just . . . it doesn't feel right."

Jonathan returned with the box. He held it victoriously over his head like a prize and yelled, "Ha! Most of the cakes are still in here. A few have bite marks, but Grandma Z. brushes the poodles' teeth. I say they're edible."

The rest of the group went to see just how bad the damage was to the cakes, but Nestor stayed back and he motioned for Robyn to hold back too.

He said softly, "You know, you can keep coming, even when Sundae learns the seesaw. You could join our regular class, even. Sundae could be a demonstration dog, like Fudge. And I could use a co-teacher. Jonathan and Alejandra are good helpers, but they don't have your experience."

Robyn took the tip of her shoe and made an arc in the patch of dirt she was standing in. There was Nestor being Nestor again: seeing things that other people missed. She had to admit it; he was onto something. Maybe part of her didn't want Sundae to compete because she didn't want him to finish with this extra training. If he could do the seesaw, if he didn't need Fudge's emotional support while doing the course, then where would that leave Robyn? She'd be out of ability once more. She'd be returning to pick up Fudge just when everyone else was gone or leaving.

But that wasn't all of it, because she had handball now, and recess, and sometimes, still, even tutoring in the media center with Emily and goofy, unpredictable Harrison. She didn't think she'd lose all that she'd gotten back if Sundae learned to do the whole obstacle course by himself. She wouldn't let herself.

She thanked Nestor for the offer. She really did appreciate it, and the thought of helping Nestor teach anything? Nothing sounded better. But as for competing, she still had the same feeling she'd had before. Something about it just didn't sit right. Something about it felt wrong.

And then she ran into Lulu and Marshan.

Robyn and Mom had gone to a restaurant in the center of town. They had a sidewalk table and the dogs were seated beneath it.

Lulu and Marshan came walking down the street with Lulu's mother. They had just gotten out of their sewing class and each of them was carrying a little wicker case full of sewing supplies.

As soon as they saw Robyn, they ran to her and said hi.

Lulu's mom had met Robyn's mother a few times before, and now the adults fell into talking as Lulu pulled her latest creation out of her sewing case. Lulu had made a wraparound skirt for herself—blue with little yellow flowers. It was a real step up from the cat clothes Robyn had seen pictures of. The seams were perfectly straight. It looked like something a person might actually wear, and she told that to Lulu.

Lulu beamed as Marshan explained that something had gone terribly wrong with the skirt she herself was making. She pulled a puckered square of fabric out of her case and showed Robyn a tight ball of thread in the middle of it. "I blame the sewing machine," she said. "It's a clunker."

Sundae popped out from under the table, and Lulu and Marshan began to coo.

"Look, it's poor little Fudgey," said Marshan.

Lulu squinted sympathetically. "How is she doing?"

Mom looked over at them. "Hold on," she said. "Is something wrong with Fudge?"

"This is actually Sundae," said Robyn. "And nothing

is wrong with Fudge. Fudge is fine."

Mom shrugged and returned to her conversation with Lulu's mom, who said she was in a hurry to drop off Marshan so that she and her family could have dinner of their own. So they all said their goodbyes, and Robyn and Mom watched Lulu, her mother, and Marshan walk toward the parking lot.

Mom looked at her watch and then glanced back at the restaurant. She said, "I hope they bring dinner soon. I'm hungry."

"Me too," said Robyn.

They waited a minute more. Then Mom said, "What was that about Fudge?"

Robyn rolled her eyes. She told Mom how Lulu and Marshan were a couple of sadness tourists. "They always act like they care so much about Fudge's disabilities, but really, it's just to make them feel better about themselves."

Mom let out a long breath. "I've met people like that. They can be annoying."

"I know. It's like they only see that one part of Fudge, the part that can't see or hear. And with Sundae, it's just the opposite. They can only see the part of him that is good at agility. It's like they don't even hear me when I say how scared he can get."

"Well," said Mom, smiling now as the waiter set their food in front of them. Lasagna for Robyn. Salmon for Mom. "People do like the pretty surfaces, don't they? They like to see the winners. They like to see the beautiful. They like to see the smiles. They don't like to see the 'broken.' They don't like to see the 'weak.' And they don't like stories that complicate which is which."

Robyn swallowed a bite of her dinner and sat back in her chair. "Why?"

Mom sat back in her own chair. She shook her head. "I don't know. Maybe because eventually we all break, eventually we all get weak. People don't want to be reminded."

One of the dogs dropped its head on Robyn's foot, and through her thin sock she could feel the soft in and out of either Sundae or Fudge breathing. "But that seems so sad. Because what happens when you're not the winner or the most beautiful? Or when you make the story all complicated?"

"Indeed," said Mom.

Robyn shook her head. "No, really. What happens?"

Mom dabbed her mouth with her napkin. She blinked. "What do you think happens?"

An uncomfortable energy snaked through Robyn. "Maybe . . . something bad."

Mom nodded slowly. "Maybe. Sometimes."

And Robyn knew. That was the problem with the competition. The competition was a lie. It was just like her rules. It was a way to show one chapter of Sundae, the chapter everyone else wanted to see. The chapter everyone else wanted to celebrate. The chapter that ignored all of Sundae's wounds and all of his traumas and mistakes and was simply called "Winner." People liked that chapter. That chapter made them forget, just for a little while, about the brokenness and weakness that, eventually, claim all of us.

Well, call garbage on that.

She wasn't going to do that to Sundae. She wasn't going to make him a champion just so everyone else would feel good. She wasn't going to hide his struggles. She was going to paint them purple, like a big, neon grape. She was going to make people see that he was strong and weak. Same as Fudge. Same as her. Same as everyone. And he didn't need their pity. And he didn't need their applause. But he did need to be seen. Because he needed the pack, and the pack needed him. Whatever they thought, the pack needed the Sundaes and the Fudges. They needed them just the way they were.

And because she knew that, she knew exactly what she needed to do.

CHAPTER 24

ROBYN STOOD OUTSIDE THE convention center. Fog had rolled into town, and she was draped in mist as hundreds of people streamed by her. Her dogs stood at her side, as did Mom and Nivien.

Dad was on video chat.

"How are you feeling?" he asked.

"Good," she said.

"More importantly, how is Sundae feeling?" asked Mom.

Robyn looked down at Sundae. His tail was partly down, and he kept sitting and then standing, and then nuzzling into Fudge.

"He's nervous," said Robyn. "But he's not overly nervous. I think he's going to be okay."

Out of the fog stepped Lulu and Marshan. They each held a triangular flag that had GO, SUNDAE! written in bright glitter glue.

"Hey," they said upon seeing Robyn. "This is so cool."

They knelt and petted Sundae. "Poor little Sundae," they cooed. "Robyn told us how scared you were. But you don't have to be scared. It's all going to be okay. We're going to be right there cheering for you."

Robyn thanked them for coming and said she'd see them in the convention hall.

As they left, Dad said, "Who was that? How come they didn't say anything to Fudge?"

Out of the corner of her mouth, Robyn said, "They have vision impairments of their own."

Nivien squeezed Robyn's shoulder. "But we're just going to worry about our own eyesight, right?"

Robyn reached up and touched Nivien's arm. "Right."

More and more people were streaming into the building now, and Mom asked if they should head over to the sign-in area.

But Robyn wanted to wait as long as possible. Sundae needed her, and he needed Fudge, but she knew now that he also needed his whole goofy pack. Together, they'd give him the strength he'd need.

She said goodbye to Dad, and here they came, a few of them at a time. Alejandra, William, and Tiger. Harrison and Strudel. Emily and Max, and the rest of the ability class. They grouped around her.

"I'm nervous," said Emily.

"Me too," said William.

"Don't be nervous," said Alejandra. "It's going to be great."

Finally, Nestor and Jonathan appeared, and behind them came Mrs. Zazueta, Gigante, and even Bruce.

"So . . . we gonna do this?" said Nestor.

"We're gonna do this," said Robyn.

They walked into the arena, Mrs. Zazueta and Gigante leading the way. They reached the check-in area, and Mrs. Zazueta went up to the attendant. She spoke for a while, and then the attendant's face brightened. "Yes," she said. "We've been expecting you. Follow me."

They followed the attendant to a private area of the arena, where they were told to wait.

They looked out at the obstacle course. A chocolate Lab, as perfect a dog specimen as ever lived, was running it. They watched him go: hurdle, hurdle, dog walk, tunnel, A-frame, pause table, seesaw, weave poles, second dog walk, second tunnel, exit box. He was spectacular. Fast. Precise. Confident. Happy. He was what an agility-trained dog should be.

"That was good," said Robyn.

"That was amazing," said Alejandra. "But that dog has got nothing on us."

Mrs. Zazueta looked at everyone. "Are you ready?"

Robyn nodded, and she felt the collective nods of all her friends and even all the dogs.

An announcer called Mrs. Zazueta to the arena.

She walked to the center, and she moved with such sureness that the room grew quiet. An attendant brought her a microphone.

She looked out at the crowd. She said she had been training dogs and competing with them in agility for over thirty years and that some of the happiest, proudest moments of her life had been spent in that very ring. "But," she said, pausing, "we haven't seen what it means to be truly *agile*—to be truly clever and fast and nimble. Today, we'd like to rectify that with a special demonstration." She explained briefly about Nestor's class, about what they had been doing, how they had gotten started, and how all of them, together, had invented this new sport, this sport that showcased the strengths and challenges of every dog, of every handler.

"Friends and dog lovers," she said. "I give you . . . *ability* training."

The entire ability-training class lined up near the entrance box, and one by one, each dog was directed through the course. First Tiger, who, on three legs, raced through the obstacles, happily barking the entire time, even as he expertly made his way across the dog walk. The old pug and the old pit bull came next. Then Strudel, who didn't fall asleep once. Then Emily, who stood on her braces in the middle of the course and directed Max from device to device with purely verbal commands, and after Max was done, up stepped Nestor and Bruce, wild Bruce, unpredictable, lurching and lunging Bruce, who, when he was done, leaped onto Jonathan and pinned him to the ground.

Some of the dogs did every obstacle, and some needed a team of helpers, and some moved fast, and some moved slow. But each of them enchanted the crowd, not because they defied everyone's expectations— although many of them did—but because they showed the breadth, depth, and sheer commonness of talent and grit that existed if only people were willing to look.

Finally, it was Robyn's turn as handler. She walked into the entrance box with Sundae and Fudge. And with Fudge and her helpers leading the way, she led both her dogs through the course. And no one saw how fast Sundae could actually run. And no one saw how high Sundae could actually leap. But everyone saw what really mattered: Real champions don't need to go it alone. Real champions don't even need medals. Real champions find a way. And in the darkness, they follow the scent of their pack.

ACKNOWLEDGMENTS

Dear Reader:

Thank you for reading this book. It means so much to me that—of all the things you could have done—you decided to spend your time with Robyn, Sundae, Fudge, and all the people and dogs in their world.

I hope that one day I'll be reading a story that you wrote. And when I do, I'll know that a lot of people helped you bring that story to life. They helped you by believing in you and encouraging you to work harder than you knew you could. You know who did that for me? My editor, Alex Borbolla. Oh, boy. She did not let me slack off at all. Thank goodness! This book is so much better because of her insights and criticisms. It's also better because of Mary Finnegan, who likewise read and critiqued this work, and because of Tracy Marchini, who always advocates for my writing.

Other people helped bring this book to life too. The amazing Karyn Lee has designed all my books—and this time she also illustrated the cover, and I hope you'll agree with me in thinking that it is one of the cutest covers ever! Thank you, Karyn! And thank you, Kaitlyn San Miguel and the copy editors and proofreaders, including the talented Ariel So, who found the many mistakes and errors that my eyes just glazed right past. And thank you also to the marketing team at Simon Kids, as well as Sarah Shealy and Barbara Fisch at Blue Slip Media, who always work hard to get my work on the radar of readers.

Writers need more than a team of people helping them put out good work. They also need time . . . to . . . write. The only reason I had enough time to finish this book was because my good friends Alexandria Levitt and Teresa Atwater each gave me a room to hide away in and write when that was what I really needed. So I hope that when you're writing your story, you will find people who will do the same. Because time and a quiet room are the two things writers cannot do without.

But even when you share your story, your life will always be more than your writing, so I hope you will always have lots of people who love you and think you're awesome. My family, especially my husband, Steve, my daughters, my amazing Soup Club Ladies, my Camp Scripps friends, and my colleagues at Cal

State LA always make me feel awesome, and I feel so lucky to have them in my life.

Last but not least, I cross my fingers that, one day, you will have a dog who jumps on your desk at three o'clock every afternoon and reminds you that it's time to play ball, or at least take a belly-rub break. I have a dog like that. His name is Walt. And I appreciate him very much.